BETRAYAL

Adriaan van Dis

Translated from the Dutch by Ina Rilke

MACLEHOSE PRESS
QUERCUS · LONDON

First published in the Dutch language as *Tikkop*
by Uitgeverij Augustus, Amsterdam in 2010
First published in Great Britain in 2013 by

MacLehose Press
an imprint of Quercus
55 Baker Street
7th Floor, South Block
London W1U 8EW

This book was published with the support of
the Dutch Foundation for Literature

N ederlands
N letterenfonds
dutch foundation
for literature

A CIP catalogue record for this book is available
from the British Library.

ISBN (HB) 978 0 85705 184 4
ISBN (TPB) 978 0 85705 185 1
ISBN (Ebook) 978 1 78087 075 5

BETRAYAL

need to take pills. Mulder did, eight a day. Still, he might as well try to raise himself to Marten's standards. Maybe the name would make him young again.

He opened the windows wide, filled his lungs with sea air, and resolved to make the sitting room a bit more habitable: table up against the wall, sofa by the window, knick-knacks in the cupboards and surplus chairs to the scullery. Freeing up some space for his legs and his eyes.

The house stood on the crest of a sand-dune, overlooking the fishing village and the harbour. That was where he had wanted to live, down by the shore in a village where people worked for their living, not among the high-walled villas of idle whites with electrified fencing glinting in the sun. Just an ordinary little house on the beachfront, was that really so hard to find, especially out of season?

He had discussed the matter at length with Donald by e-mail and phone. "You seem to be on pretty good terms with the fishing community, don't you ever hear of anything? Don't you ever see anything vacant when you're out with the dogs?" He had declined the offer of lodging with his old friend, who lived in the largest house on the dunes. Staying in other people's homes did not appeal to Mulder: too much embarrassment, too many pills and too many rituals. Plus he would have to carry on conversations with Donald's wife, whom he had never even met. "Looking someone up after forty years means it takes a while to get back in the swing of things." People change, like it or not.

After much asking around, Donald had found him an "authentic fisherman's cottage, nets and boats all around, less than a minute from the sea." Great, Mulder had promptly gone out to buy a pair of rubber boots. But a week before his departure it all fell through.

Donald had spoken to the previous occupants: they had been on the point of going to bed when they were robbed at knifepoint by youths in balaclavas. Fleeced of everything, even their tooth brushes. "Crime is spreading like a disease over the country," Donald wrote. "It has reached the fishing village, too. I can't let you live there. Oldies like you and me belong in a safe area. We can't run as fast as we used to. I'll find you somewhere else."

So now he was lumbered with this draughty dump in a white enclave. The view was splendid, admittedly. A pity that everybody had an equally splendid view of him. Unsurprisingly, his arrival had not gone unnoticed. As Donald drove him up the winding track there had already been a bunch of fishermen's children running alongside the 4x4. As if they had been lying in wait for the new tenant. They swarmed around him as he unloaded his luggage. "Mister Marten! Mister Marten!" one of them yelled. Somebody at the rental office had obviously blabbed. Donald wanted to chase the youngsters away, but he – kindly Mr Marten – had shaken hands with them as they squabbled over his suitcase. The smallest ones clamoured for a biro "for school". He patted his pockets self-consciously, but one urchin beat him to it and, grinning widely, handed over his fountain pen. His pocket picked under his very nose! Donald hustled him into the house. No, this was no game, it was a test. "Now they know how fokken dumb you are." Those innocent-looking lads were fully-fledged thieves. Hadn't he seen their sticks? Those broom-handles with a nail driven through one end, which they trailed behind them over the asphalt? If you didn't watch out they'd use them to prise open a window and fish the house keys right off the table. Donald advised him to keep the front door locked at all times even when he was at home, even during the day. And it might be a good idea to defrost that freezer so he could

9

hide his valuables in there. It was just an idea. Mulder had to laugh, but Donald didn't think it was funny. "Just you mark my words, they'll be back, and not for a friendly chat either."

Six keys lay on the table. Menacingly. A bundle of rust to scare him. He weighed them in his right hand. No idea which one belonged where. He tried them all. Half of them didn't fit anywhere, and the key to the front door required some force. A shiver ran down his spine as he slipped the keys into his trouser pocket – he felt like his own jailer. He inspected the chisel marks in the windowsill. There were greasy fingerprints on the glass. He tried to rub them off with his handkerchief. His spittle squeaked. The fingerprints were on the outside.

The freezer hummed. Mulder pulled out the plug.

The cable of the laptop was too short. The front room had only two electrical sockets, and the nearest one was already in service with hundreds of ants crawling in and out. Small red slaves politely greeting each other in passing. He went down on his knees and blew them away. They fell over each other, recovered themselves and proceeded in single file towards the socket. The route was fixed. When he covered the two entrances with his fingers the ants massed together on the back of his hand. They didn't bite, merely explored his knuckles, the scar between thumb and forefinger, the creased skin. They ventured onto his wrist, tasted the hairs, his watch strap . . . they crept up the tunnel of his sleeve. There was a crumb on the floor. Mulder laid it carefully among the ants. The ants assessed the gift, lifted it up and hauled it straight through the multitude towards the blocked entrances of the socket. Minutes ticked by, filled with wonder, endearment and cruel thoughts: he pinched an ant between his fingertips, just one, and squashed it with his nails for the juice, for the heck of it. He dropped the corpse back into the queue. His watch couldn't tell him how many minutes had elapsed – the glass was red with ants.

There was no alternative: he had to push the table over to the other socket, up close to the sofa and the window. That way he could watch the boats putting out to sea from behind his keyboard.

M ulder stared vacantly out of the window, tired from the journey. He had refused all offers of help settling in. It was nobody's business how neatly he folded his trousers over a hanger – the crease, the crease, in Africa of all places! – nor the number of shirts he had brought. Not to mention the pills. He wanted to find his way around on his own the first day. His way around the house, around the village. In his own time. He would be meeting Donald in the morning for his first long walk in the area. That would give him a different perspective, no doubt, and he would also be meeting Sarah, Donald's wife.

But first the sink had to be scraped clean, the rooms swept, and a rug draped over the sofa to hide the hideous upholstery. During his search for bedding he had stumbled on a box of newspapers and magazines left behind by previous tenants. Reading material for rainy days, news from umpteen summers ago. He was about to throw the box away, but couldn't resist riffling through the old papers – a whole stack of yellowed crime and political infighting. He stared at the photos of black government ministers, badly lit, drowned in printing ink. They wore stiff suits, sat behind desks sporting little flags. He recognised faces from the old days – so he thought, so he hoped – men he had met in the flesh, only younger, in another world. The world in which he had been Marten. Strange past, even stranger present.

Marten. How many people had known him by that name? Twenty or so at the most, he reckoned, eight of whom would have been women. It was as Marten that he had been trained in Paris, groomed for a mission to South Africa. In the winter of 1972, a young student called Mulder flew to Johannesburg, sweaty-palmed, travelling on his own passport and entering the country without any trouble. The customs officer was so pleased to see the well-thumbed Bible poking out of his hand luggage that the big suitcase got a dismissive wave. Meneer could proceed (with the most pious of looks on his face). Past Immigration he played Marten again, with whom a second Bible slipped into the country: this one hollowed out and containing false passports.

Marten the hero. Especially after a drink or two.

That same Marten had been Mulder's constant companion ever since – that is, until he fell apart a couple of years ago, one night in Paris. It wasn't only Marten crashing to pieces, it was Mulder's whole life. His words had come tumbling out of the bookcase as he slept. All the shelves broken, the floor strewn with letters, letters that no longer resembled words. Letters without sense. Close enough to touch. He wanted to pick them up, but they slipped from his grasp. A few hours later he rang a girlfriend to tell her about his weird dream. She couldn't understand what he was saying. Had he been drinking? She was alarmed and consulted a neurologist friend, who promptly sounded him out. Same story. "You're not making sense," he had said. An hour later Mulder was admitted to La Salpêtrière. A stroke. His second.

After little more than a week he was beginning to make some sense again – in Dutch. First the rhythms came back; the spelling took much longer. He sat for days with an old dictionary on his lap because he couldn't come up with the first letter of a particular word, while the sound of it zoomed in his head. Within a month his native language was once again lined up on the shelf. French was more problematic. The unwritten language seemed especially hard to reclaim. The French to do with love. Terrified of losing it for good, he spent days drifting along the boulevards and sitting behind young couples on pavement cafés, taking in their happiness. And so their words nourished his memory.

Only South Africa remained patchy.

He was still in pretty bad shape that afternoon when he went to the newly opened Musée du Quai Branly, where he was waylaid by a tall man: "Aren't you Marten? Marten the Dutchman?"

Marten? Mulder savoured the name and gave a start: yes, that was a name from way back. But who on earth was this man grabbing his right hand and kneading the scar between the thumb and index finger?

"I stitched up that wound, remember? It's me, Donald."

Donald! Another name that rang a bell. And in a flash he was back at that table, sitting next to the Algerian stamp-forger, seeing the gouge shooting into his thumb. Donald had staunched the wound. Donald from South Africa, with whom he roamed the streets of Paris, with whom he holed up in attic rooms, committing secret codes to memory. The Donald he wrote letters to in *encre sympathique* – the term for invisible ink came rushing back to him. Donald, son of a prominent Afrikaner who had broken with his family and now worked as a cleaner in a hospital to pay for his medical training. Clever Donald, serious Donald, grinning Donald, yes, he was the one who had stitched up the wound with a filched operating needle and sterile thread from a glass ampoule.

How long had they been in Paris together?

Months, months.

And how long ago was that?

They counted the years, leaping back and forth in time, shutting their eyes . . . thirty-seven, no, it had to be thirty-eight years ago. And here they were, face to face again. What a coincidence! Or was Africa the magnet, the dark heart of the museum, where both men were drawn to a dimly lit mask from Gabon – ghostly yellow, with the high cheekbones and almond eyes of a Bushman.

The name Fraternité cropped up, with a sigh and a smile. Fraternité, the organisation preparing them for underground activities in South Africa. Donald, excited, groped for the language they used to share, a mix of Afrikaans, French and English. "Hey, remember the friends we had, the tricks we played . . . and the booze? *Et cette vampe de la filature?*" He meant the puss-in-boots who taught them the art of stalking and shadowing. "Didn't you make tracks for her bed?"

Mulder chuckled, although he wasn't sure who or what was being referred to. The wrong faces flashed past, mean-looking, fanatical. There wasn't much time for recollection, anyway. Donald's wife was with him; she was waiting in the museum restaurant.

"Have you been back at all?" Donald said.

"No."

"Why not?"

"Too complicated," he said. "My memory's not too good these days."

Donald looked surprised. His mobile rang softly. A text message from his wife. What was keeping him?

They exchanged addresses hurriedly, smiling at each other's

15

real surnames – information that had been taboo during the Struggle. Everybody had an alias, some nondescript forename. Donald had kept his ever since – it belonged to the new South Africa. To Donald, the Dutch student he had known all those years ago was still simply Marten.

Marten was from Amsterdam, right?

"Yes, but living in Paris now." (Marten, Marten, amazing how snugly the name still fitted, a Danish name bestowed on him by the boss of Fraternité, on account of his pink skin and northern accent.) Yes, Paris, for several years now . . . Best decision he'd made since his first stroke: "You've got to use the time you have left to do the things you always wanted to do."

Donald nodded, a look of concern crossing his face. It was his last day there, otherwise they could have gone for a drink together. He was tied up with a medical conference, and had a formal dinner that evening.

Ah, so he had taken his degree in the end? Mulder had to suppress an overwhelming need to confide all his ailments. His unreliable memory . . . could a stroke announce itself in a dream? Oh, there was so much he wanted to ask.

The same was true of Donald. Was Marten still in touch with anyone from back then? No? Never run into anyone by chance? Not even at some demonstration or other?

"I've put all that well behind me," Mulder said. "I never was much of a political animal, you know."

Donald's mobile went off again. He made a helpless gesture. "Married?"

No, no. Mulder made the same gesture: "Well, I suppose I'm married to my freedom."

He laughed. "So nothing's changed."

And Donald? Kids?

No, no. He glanced quickly at his text message.

They would be in touch by e-mail, or rather, why didn't Marten come over to South Africa – since he was a free agent? Good exercise for the brain. A chance to see what had become of their dream, too.

Their dream, their hazardous dream. Money was what they needed – to smuggle people out of South Africa. And passports – false or real – to provide exiles with new names and new nationalities. They broke into the homes of embassy staff, planted listening devices, hid microfilms in hollowed-out Bibles . . . all stuff they had learned together and put into practice together. Mulder thought he had forgotten most of it, but the e-mails they exchanged brought it all back . . . How he had managed to rack up thousands of dollars on behalf of Fraternité by looting a medieval manuscript. *Pour la cause.* Mulder felt the old thrill again. He went back to being Marten, word for word. He needed to type out his memories to put them into some sort of order.

> *Bibliothèque Nationale. I wonder if they would still know me at the rue Richelieu: the eager medievalist in owlish glasses, shirt buttoned up to the collar, unruly hair carefully slicked back? Maps were what I was after, ancient manuscripts. But they would only let me see the microfiches. I abided by the rules. Handed in my briefcase and my pen in exchange for a government-issue pencil and ditto notebook. I gained access to an ancient world, the first contours of America – the Vinland map for Norse seafarers in search of the land of wine. And a beautiful sixteenth-century map of Mozambique Island with a Dutch cemetery*

marked on it. Couldn't they possibly let me see the real thing? I pleaded, gave them a spiel about desperately wanting to make a copy of the map so that I could show it to some tragic refugee from the island. Ah, to do that I needed an official letter of introduction. I provided it myself, complete with letterhead and rubber stamp. Because you had given me the address of a printing workshop run by an Algerian, a former F.L.N. guy, who could forge letterheads from all over the world. We opted for the University of Coimbra – ready in one day. It was you who taught me the secret of faking the imprint of rubber stamps.

After a few days of waiting I was taken aside by the library clerk. "Le pauvre nègre de Mozambique" was to get preferential treatment. The map wasn't worth a great deal anyway. I was issued with a pair of white cotton gloves and ushered into a separate room. And there, among the scholars, I won their trust. They showed me their treasures, parchments, codices, manuscripts, each one more precious than the last, served up between sheets of tissue paper in a linen box.

An American medievalist had been there for weeks, poring over the find of his life: an Old French didactic poem illustrated with a globe and two little figures meeting each other upside down. Proof, according to him, that people in the Middle Ages already believed the earth to be round, not flat. Worth ten thousand dollars in New York, easy, he said. As if he could smell my intention.

After he left I applied for access to the same Old French manuscript. As colourful as I knew the interior to be, so dull and unassuming was the exterior – a nondescript nineteenth-century red leather cover. It took me less than an hour to find an almost identical cover at a second-hand bookstall along the Seine.

Making the switch was a mere bagatelle. Applied for the number, took the box and found a seat as near as possible to the librarian on duty. (Your tip, too: no skulking in quiet corners. Brazen and upfront is less conspicuous.) Pencil in hand, notebook at the ready, stared at the parchment long and hard. Then slid the leather cover out from under the high-buttoned shirt and into the box. Slid the parchment poem up the shirt. Skin on skin. Returned the box to the librarian, who didn't bother to raise the lid. They never checked, I had noticed. Dutifully handed in pencil and note paper on the way out. A week later I flew to South Africa and you to New York. "Pour la cause."

After a fortnight's e-mail silence Donald returned the typed story. *"Not accurate."*

Not accurate? Mulder promptly hunted in all his drawers – his paper memory would soon prove that he was right. He wasn't stupid! Stuffed between some old vaccination booklets and (fake) letters of introduction he found three out-of-date passports: one Dutch, one Belgian and one South African. Identical photographs of him, three different names. The rubber stamps still looked good, too. He peered for a moment ruefully at his curly hair. To his surprise he also came across a batch of letters written in lilac ink, faded with time. Forbidden notes, sent to him in South Africa. He skimmed through them and felt again the fear of those days. The fear of giving the game away. One letter stood out from the rest: proof that the theft of the manuscript had been reported in the French press at the time.

But before he had a chance to convince Donald that he was right, he received a parcel from Cape Town: sudokus ("*to increase your brain power*") and a volume of Afrikaans poems ("*to learn off by heart*"). In the note enclosed Donald suggested they take a few trips together. Sentimental journeys. Shock therapy: "*dredge up some memories, even if they're not so good. Don' t worry, there's more stuff stored up in your brain than you think. See if we can blow away some of those cobwebs.*"

Memories that weren't so good. Well, Mulder would wait and see. He would do some mental exercise – the offer was there, after all! That same afternoon he stopped off at Au Vieux Campeur to buy a small rucksack. For the trips within the trip. Memory excursions.

A helicopter flew overhead and hovered above the fishing village. Birds took cover in the bushes. The open windows shook in the wind. The hinges were loose. Having found a tool box in the scullery, Mulder tried tightening the screws. He also secured the window frame with a couple of long nails.

Two hammer blows later a large, blowsy woman appeared on his doorstep: breathless, distraught, clutching her mobile, sunglasses pushed up into her blonde hair. His neighbour from across the road. "Ah, you must be the new tenant! I was afraid the place was being burgled. Did you hear that helicopter just now? The police are doing a raid. I saw the skollies running off in all directions. They were at it again last night, threw a stone in our pool, and squirted resin in the lock on the other neighbours' gate." Her eyes darted about, scanning nervously for intruders. "Yes, well, you've got to be careful in the daytime, too."

Mulder pointed to the nails in the window frame: "I'm taking precautions."

"But you'd left it wide open a while ago."

She apologised for her unceremonious entrance. "That noise from the helicopter, whirr-whirr – it makes me so nervous." She had a little bump on her nose. It trembled.

Mulder reassured her: " It's alright, I was at home."

"But you weren't in the room just now," she said, shaking her head. "That computer – is that where you keep it, on the table?"

No, he was going to defrost the freezer.

"The freezer?" She clapped her hand to her mouth. "But that's the first place they go looking. They want food as well, you know."

She had a better idea: the washing machine. In the drum, couple of sheets on top, switch on standby.

Standby? Mulder stared at her, glassy-eyed.

"So the lid automatically locks."

And where was he thinking of hiding his credit card when he went to the beach? And his passport?

Mulder glanced around the room. "Tuck them behind a picture?"

Wrong again. They expected to find safes hidden behind pictures. The Bible was the best place. Did he have one? Thieves were scared to death of the Bible. They might be wicked, but they were believers. And he should ask the landlord for some new light bulbs. Yes, hadn't he noticed? The bulbs were missing from the outside lamps. Unscrewed before his arrival, happened all the time. School kids, first thing they learnt. He'd have to put brackets over the lights. Or barbed wire – which was what she had done herself.

Would he fancy coming over for a drink later on? Sundowner, meet the neighbours. The men would be able to give him better advice than her.

He thanked her for the invitation. "Very kind of you to keep an eye out for me."

Mulder liked the sense of risk, the flirting with danger. When swimming in the sea he held his breath until he almost choked, until the blood pounded behind his ears and he saw himself in a film – his life flashing past. He let himself float, feeling alive.

Danger kept you sharp. He had read up a lot about South Africa in the papers lately, in preparation for this trip. What was going on there? All those anxious whites. Wasn't it just a lot of scaremongering, people wallowing in their fear? Risks were there to be taken. Nothing ventured, nothing gained. Hadn't Donald and he trained together to face danger?

Perhaps he should go and look for a place to live himself, to exorcise the fear, his fear and Donald's. Wasn't that something he owed to his former self? To the Marten who had learned to survive in the wilderness, in theory as well as practice, crawling on his belly through the mud with a dagger between his teeth. Marten the impostor, the forger. That Marten was alive and kicking. Comrade Marten was not a sick man.

There was nothing in the house: no bread, no coffee, no eggs. And just one mean roll of toilet paper. Donald had offered to drive him to the nearest township – a good hour by car. "Distriksdorp is where everybody goes for supplies." The fishers too? No, they had their own stores.

"Then I'll do my shopping there," Mulder had said. He was determined to find his own bearings, and the more so when Donald heaved a demonstrative sigh.

Mulder slung the rucksack over his shoulders and went down to the settlement behind the harbour. A boat was putting out to sea, the white surf crashed on the pier. The harbour was deserted, and turned out, on closer inspection, to consist of little more than a concrete ramp on a dirty stretch of beach. What was left of the fishing fleet lay rusting in the sun, rigging slapping against masts.

He caught the smell of fried fish, heard children's voices, saw a plume of smoke. Past the cold store he found his first shop, a wooden shack where they sold fish. A woman was frying squid. She offered him a ring – fried bicycle tyre – and he bought a portion in a plastic tray. Children jostled around him, a ragged crowd in bare feet or flip-flops, too young and too small to roam white neighbourhoods causing trouble, but cheeky enough to ask him for money and gawp at his every movement: Hey, the foreigner's eating with his fingers, the foreigner's chewing, he's chewing for a very long time, he's taking out a handkerchief, wiping his lips, blowing his nose. They nudged each other, couldn't get enough of him. Mulder ordered a portion of squid for them and handed the tray to the oldest girl. Wordlessly, like an offering. She shared out the rings like a young mother. He listened to the children as they ate, trying to catch the melody of their Afrikaans – as though tuning his own voice – but when he asked them a question he got it all wrong and they ran off.

Beyond the cold store the settlement fanned out in rising rows of identical dwellings, facing inwards and away from the sea. Picturesque at first sight, orderly. The main track even had a few front-room shops – dealers in air time, top-up cards for mobile phones and the like. A weather-beaten woman was selling bread – spongy white loaves in plastic bags. Her toothless next-door neighbour was selling jars of home-made jam. He asked about the flavours, but couldn't make out what she mumbled.

Pleased with his first purchases, he decided to walk on, towards the sprawl of concrete further inland. The path narrowed and dipped, with piles of fishing net on either side, trails of seaweed, agricultural plastic, empty bottles. As though the sea had disgorged its waste all the way into the village. The walls felt damp. He heard thumping behind closed shutters, blaring radios, crying infants. Now and then he had to jump over puddles of brackish water. It stank of piss and shit. His trousers were getting spattered. (He needed to buy washing powder! A decent scrubbing brush!)

The further he went, the shabbier the houses. Only the small churches stood proud. The prayer hall was decorated with shells, though the Pentecostal centre was windowless. The school had burnt to the ground. The lampposts, too, had been wrecked, but the electric cables remained: sagging festoons looping from one zinc roof to the next. He kicked an empty flat-screen T.V. box out of his way. A dazed woman stood at an open window, her baby lying unshielded in the sun. A teenager staggered outside from the dark into the light, mumbling to himself and screwing up his eyes.

Mulder had taken a step too far, looking directly into the poverty and seeing things not meant for his eyes. When it came down to it, his curiosity always got the better of him. Moreover he was now lost and could no longer hear the sound of the surf. His head throbbed and his throat was parched. He looked around for a hovel or an open door. On a patch of wasteland he spotted a leaking pump. Two dogs were drinking the spilt water. He went over to them, put his head under the tap, slurping, snorting. A pebble dropped into the mud beside him. And another. He felt something hit his rucksack, swung round and found himself eye to eye with a crowd of youngsters. Deathly quiet. Arms akimbo. They had crept up on him. The kids from the fried squid stand – they must have taken a different route. Their eyes took note of his clothing, his dripping collar, the stains on his trousers, the mud on his shoes. Leather shoes.

"Where do you all live?" he said.

No answer – just wider eyes.

The girl he had given the fried squid to stepped forward. She looked at him intently, took his hand and led him up a grassy slope.

25

The other children trooped after them, excitedly. The girl pointed out the path to the sea.

It was a hint. An order.

He walked as fast as he could towards the sound of the surf, without looking back, clambering over low walls and piles of rubbish. After a maze of backyards and alleys he no longer heard voices, but no surf either. He had shaken off the kids, and stood behind a small house to get his breath back. A woman came out, wild-eyed, her face painted white, her dress torn. She held a lifeless puppy over her shoulder and began to laugh noiselessly.

The sun was already setting behind the dunes. Over the next hillock he found the youngsters waiting for him again. They had been joined by some older boys. They grinned. The boldest among them had had their front teeth pulled. They were in high spirits, stamping their feet in the mud. Not a knife or stick in sight. He wanted to turn back, heard a vague growling noise, and suddenly felt a fiery pain in his calf. There was a dog hanging on to his trouser leg, a fat, snarling dachshund that wouldn't let go. "Go for it! Go for it!" yelled the boys. Mulder couldn't get away, the dachshund tightened its grip. Kicking and screaming had no effect. His trouser leg turned red. "Let loose!", someone shouted. "Down, dog!" A gangly youth with tattoos came forward. The dachshund slunk away.

He set off again as if nothing had happened, fighting the pain, ankle-deep in mud, past a couple of drunks. Only when he felt the soft sand of the dunes underfoot did he dare to look down at his leg. Bloodstains all over. He kicked off his shoes and limped over to the beach to wash the wound in the sea – four little holes rinsed open, deep and pink, just above the heel. The salt water stung. His trouser leg was ripped, but his skin was only punctured. He waded further into the sea to wash the fright off his face.

The youngsters stood on the top of the dune, watching. Mulder straightened up – they were not to see him in pain.

There was a trail of blood spots along the harbour. A spot every two paces, glistening in the sunshine. The trail curved up towards the villas on the dunes. Ants gorged themselves, black beetles came running for a taste. Unaware of leaving traces, Mulder strode ahead like a soldier, commandeering his stiff right leg. It was only when he turned his toilet-bag upside down in the bathroom that he noticed anything. He was standing in a pool of blood, his sock was soaked through. Had he really forgotten to bring any plasters? All he had was cholesterol inhibitors, blood pressure lowering medication and three different sorts of memory-improvement pills. Also foil strips of anti-malaria drugs and water purification tablets (out of date) – all the stuff one takes on an African journey – but it hadn't occurred to him to bring a simple box of assorted plasters or even a bottle of iodine. He wrapped a sock around his calf and tied a handkerchief around that. Cushion under the leg and a glass of duty-free whisky as painkiller. Full to the brim and a drop extra for the ants.

Sundowner time. The neighbours from up the hill and next door came past, armed with bottles and snacks in Tupperware. Mulder ducked away from the window and hobbled to the bathroom. There were voices, knocks on the door, someone rattling the gate at the back, but no-one could see him sitting in the bathroom reading old newspapers with his leg propped up on the side of the bathtub, glass of whisky in hand, next to the washing machine, where his laptop was playing hide-and-seek in his blood-stained trousers. Mulder waited for nightfall, so he could go and lie down on the sitting-room sofa and look at the stars, search out the Southern Cross – the way he used to do in the bad old days. But his stomach was playing up. Pills didn't help. He thought to smother the heartburn with bread and jam. He wolfed down half a loaf of white bread. Darkness fell rapidly, but the kids came back to haunt him and he was obliged to sleep sitting bolt upright in bed.

Mulder woke up not knowing where he was. In which country, which year. There appeared to be dogs barking at his bedside. And that commotion in the background? Someone was calling his name, his new old name. It was Donald on the stoep, Mulder's flaky front porch. He came straight into the house, without waiting for an answer. He wore shorts. The door wasn't locked: how could Marten be so stupid? Come on, get dressed, get a move on. Nothing better for the brain than a brisk walk. The morning had to be taken advantage of. The dolphins came past at this hour. Quick.

Mulder limped about, putting on his clothes: T-shirt and long khaki trousers, sharply creased from lying in his suitcase. The dogs sniffed around the stoep nervously. Donald pointed to a red smear.

"Jam," Mulder said. An accident with the jamjar. He had no wish for further injunctions.

They both fiddled with the lock on the front door. The fifth key fitted. Meanwhile, the dogs poked their noses in his crotch. A French custom, according to Donald, they were pedigree *chiens d' Artois*, hand-picked in Picardy by his wife and flown over.

They took the sandy path behind the villas and climbed up the wild dunes, with Donald in the lead. Mulder kept sliding back and soon lagged behind. His leg was hurting, but he said nothing.

He was surprised by the amount of sand their feet kicked up, and by how far down the fishing village actually was. So exposed, so vulnerable to heavy rains and spring tides. Donald referred to it as the under-village. Had the fishers settled there of their own accord? No, Donald said, previously their homes were up in the dunes, but then apartheid came and all the fishing folk were made to go and live down by the harbour. "Social Reconstruction" was what this was called, ostensibly so they would be closer to their boats. All neat and tidy in rows, they would be spared the climb and there would be less noise in the night. But what it was really about was the rich having an unobstructed view from their windows. "Your place used to be called the kaffir house – the only building from the old days that wasn't razed to the ground."

The harbour glittered in the morning sunlight. From up here you could clearly see the no-man's-land between the white neighbourhood and the coloured – a flat stretch of thistles and stunted, windblown trees. A division which, according to Donald, had only been mitigated after the changeover, by the construction of a hotel.

"So is it a bit mixed there now?" Mulder asked.

No, the manager was Portuguese, an exile from Mozambique. "The colour bar goes right up to his skull."

Mulder stopped asking questions, although he was curious about the burnt-out school, the shacks and the craziness he had seen around the backyards. What did all those people do for a living? But he didn't want to sound critical so soon after his arrival, and besides, he wanted to give Donald a chance to act as his guide – on the first day, at any rate.

They went uphill and down again, only to climb even higher dunes. After an hour Mulder felt dizzy, he thought he might faint

30

and withdrew into the bushes – supposedly for a pee – and threw up. The dogs were eager to lap up his vomit. Donald was oblivious to all this: he was gazing ecstatically at a school of dolphins swimming by.

Bays unfurled, boulders broke the waves. Now and then they came upon a patch of dark earth. Old ground. Ancestral. Donald pointed to the mounds of shells on the edge of the beach: "Shell middens, the dinner tables of the first coastal inhabitants." He had found knapped flints there – chisels and blades from prehistoric times.

The dogs bounded ahead of them, playful and yapping. They fought over a branch and then trotted off with it in tandem, each with one end in its jaws. There was a roar of engines, a cloud of powdery sand drifting by. Dune buggies ridden by young fishers on their way to remote beaches – smugglers and poachers, so Donald said. They raced over the tracks, cut across ancestral grounds.

"Keep well away from those guys." He shook his head sadly. "See that hollow beyond those rocks? Arrows have been found there," he said with forced enthusiasm. "And bones of springbok and zebra, but also of bigger animals that used to hunt for food in these parts. There were lions here once."

The dogs yawned impatiently. Donald had confiscated their shared stick to trace a figure in the sand. There was something he wanted to explain. He was always doing this back in Paris, forever drawing on paper napkins, steamed-up windows, dusty shelves. Sketchy outlines, maps unconstrained by frontiers. And now he put a small cross on the coast to indicate the place Mulder had fetched up in, where white and black had met many centuries ago – Dutch Boers from the supply station at the Cape of Good Hope in search of pastureland, and the Khoikhoi, the earliest inhabitants of the southernmost tip of Africa. Stammerers, to the ears of the first colonists: Hottentots, primitive creatures somewhere between monkey and man, too unreliable to serve as slaves.

Donald marked out the new settlements in the sand, and the vineyards belonging to the early Huguenots. Slave ships used to dock in the harbour – labour you could rely on, from Mozambique, West Africa, Madagascar, the East Indies. Mulder was glad to sit and watch, as the pain was now nagging in his groin.

Donald waved his stick in the air: "I love this place."

"Because of the past?"

"No, the future."

"Oh, that explains why you live in a white neighbourhood, I suppose. On top of a sand-dune."

Donald kicked a shell out of his path. His friend had spoiled his declaration of love.

One more lesson before breakfast. Donald drew the outline of Cape Province, marked the cattle outposts, traced the routes of the Great Trek north staged in the early nineteenth century by Boers seeking to escape government interference. Look, that was where his language was born, a bastard language, nurtured by slaves and Boers alike. No better language to describe the beauty and the hardship.

"I can't survive without it," Donald said earnestly. "That's why I came back here from the Cape, back to the roots. It's where I can keep my ears to the ground." He crossed out his drawing. "Our fishers lead a very ancient kind of life here. Rounded and worn smooth like the pebbles on the beach. The Afrikaans they speak is very beautiful. They catch all sorts of wonderful words in their nets, even if they can barely read and write. But their words don't go down too well in this day and age. Their language is contaminated. *Our* language is contaminated. Next thing, it'll be gone."

Mulder said nothing. He thought back on the sullen crowd in the under-village, but more than that he tried to picture Donald in the old days, the young South African in Paris who refused to speak Afrikaans, aside from the occasional exclamation. And yet Mulder had begged him to: oh, it had such a charming sound, and when you heard it spoken it came so much closer to Dutch than when you read it. But no, Afrikaans was kak.

Donald was afraid of hurting his black comrades' feelings. Although they called themselves and each other "laaitie", or "boy", for fun, and although they cracked the rudest jokes in Afrikaans, it was still the language of commands and insults as far as they were concerned. *Net vir blankes*, for whites only.

One time, though, after a long evening's work, when he was tipsy and there were no fellow countrymen around, Donald had burst out singing the Afrikaans national anthem: *Uit die blou van onse hemel, uit die diepte van ons see* – From the blue of our skies, from the depth of our sea. Out of tune and full of loathing, but with tears in his eyes. It was one of their small secrets. None of the comrades were supposed to know, because Donald was held to be a man of strict principles, and besides, mawkishness would only undermine the struggle. But ever since that shared moment of Donald's weakness he and Mulder had addressed each other in their respective mother tongues.

Mulder placed his foot on the erased Cape. "So you made your choice in the end."

"I was ashamed. Yes, they were cruel times. But now I'm no longer afraid to love my language ... or my country."

Donald stared at the dunes lighting up in the sunrise. "And you, is there anything you love?"

"Anything?"

The sun fell on their faces and they looked at each other, mutely.

It was dark in Donald's house. The blinds were down.

"Sarah?"

No answer. Sarah was supposed to be preparing breakfast, a welcome breakfast for their friend from overseas.

Donald swore under his breath and strode down the corridor, opening doors on his way. "Sarah?" He disappeared into a room.

Mulder waited in the kitchen, letting his eyes get used to the dark. A coffee machine gurgled, the oven clock jumped to the next digit, the fridge hummed. He heard noises at the back of the corridor, muffled and plaintive. The dogs were whining by their empty food bowls.

Donald entered the kitchen. He apologised and pulled up the blinds. The sun poured in. He paused, facing the sink. Sarah had a migraine.

They ate their bacon and eggs in silence.

The stiffness worsened. After two days Mulder was dragging his leg. The neighbour from down the road noticed at once: "Got a limp, have you?"

He mumbled something about a pulled muscle, but she wasn't letting him off so easily.

"You look washed out."

Mulder felt washed out. Reluctantly, he showed her the bite. His calf was so swollen he could barely pull up his trouser leg. A sausage dog, yes, a stupid worshond. There was a bluey-green ring around the wound. The neighbour felt the back of his knee – she used to be a nurse. "When did you last have a tetanus jab?"

Mulder couldn't remember.

"Do you feel stiff?"

"I always feel stiff."

"Your jaws, too?"

Mulder said AAAH. His lower jaw wouldn't close.

"To the doctor with you," she said briskly. Her husband was off fishing with some friends, but she could drive him. "Us neighbours help each other." She ran inside to get her bag and car keys. Mulder didn't stop her (despite shuddering at that hand behind his knee). He was all too happy to leave Donald out of it. So was she, apparently "He's hopeless, you know, a paper doctor, far too clever for everyday ailments."

For a G.P. you had to drive to Distriksdorp some hundred kilometres inland; the hospital was there too. More than an hour's drive. "We live a long way from civilisation . . . No decent shops, no pastor, no higher education, no cinema or sports ground." She gave an apologetic laugh. "Just boredom." Yes, the coloureds had a hard time of it, which was why she'd give her maid a ring first, see if she needed a lift. "You don't go to town in an empty car." It was an unwritten rule among car owners in the duneland.

"No bus service?" Mulder ventured.

"No, they tried it, but it didn't work. People prefer hitching a lift, it's cheaper."

Mulder had no idea what his neighbour's name was. Had she introduced herself to him or not? The bump on her nose had stuck in his mind, but her name?

The maid, in a pale-blue pinafore, was waiting by the hotel parking lot. She spotted the car straight away and came towards them, waving. Reaching the car out of breath, she tilted her head to a knot of bystanders hoping for a lift. Could Madam fit someone else in, too?

"You choose."

Mulder lowered the window and watched the maid walk over to three waiting women.

"Oh no, not oyster-sellers," the nose-bump neighbour groaned. "I don't want that smell in my car." But they did not want a lift, they were waiting for the hotel supplier's refrigerator truck (legs straddled over their baskets so their long skirts shielded the merchandise from the sun). They pointed to a mother with a sick child and an old woman who needed to fetch medicines for her husband.

The back doors clicked open. A skinny youth stepped forward. His right arm was wrapped in a dirty cloth, but his pink sneakers were spotless. He was contorted with pain.

"No, not him!" cried the maid. "He's an incomer."

"A skollie," the old woman chimed in. "That's what he is, a skollie going to sell stolen goods in town."

"But his arm's broken," Mulder protested. "You can see it's all crooked."

"He's putting it on," the neighbour said. "He's got a knife in that cloth." Her nose-bump had turned pale.

Mulder was surprised by the anger on her face. She pressed the automatic door-lock button, but he was already getting out of the car – her hand covering his didn't stop him. She gave him a beseeching look.

"Two pains for the price of one," he said through the open window, and limped over to the boy, out of obstinacy, aware of disapproving glances. There was no turning back.

He reached out and felt the cloth gingerly.

The boy chewed his lip.

"No knife, pockets empty too. Can he come now?"

The neighbour avoided his eyes. "Didn't you hear what she said? He's not from around here. And I'm not supposed to give lifts to strangers, unless they're fishers."

"In that case you needn't bother to take me either." Mulder was startled by his own noble attitude. "Sorry."

Red nails drummed on the steering wheel. "O.K. then, on your head be it."

"I could get in the back," Mulder said. "Then he could go next to you – any bother from him and I'd break his other arm."

"Oh, don't be absurd. I want a strong man next to me," she said crossly, twisting round to retrieve her handbag: getting four people in was going to be a squeeze. Mulder slid the passenger seat forward and bent his stiff leg. The boy groaned as he climbed into the back. He smelled of fish.

They drove into the dry hinterland. No-one spoke. He stared at her fingernails, pointed and smooth, untouched by any kind of work. A chill wind scraped the veld. The sun was pale, but surprisingly warm for the time of year. Sheep huddled together in the shade of a tree. Farmers were burning the stubble. The heat blew into the car.

The road was badly rutted, the groaning grew louder. The neighbour turned up the air conditioning and adjusted the rear-view mirror to keep an eye on the boy's face. Perspiration pearled on her upper lip. To distract her Mulder pointed to the numbers of ostriches in a field by the road.

"A farm," she said.

"Look, they're running alongside us."

"They can easily outrun a car. They're very inquisitive. I wouldn't be surprised if one of them breaks a leg. Rather accident-prone, they are," she said in English.

Her voice had soared by a fluttery octave. But why the sudden switch from Afrikaans?

"We spoke two languages at home. My mother was Afrikaans, my father British. We had an ostrich farm." She tilted her head to the back and whispered: "These fishing people are very inquisitive too, you know. I don't want them to skinder about us." Her nostrils quivered.

"They don't speak English?"

"It's not in their curriculum."

Mulder massaged his stiff jaw and looked outside again. The ostriches had dropped out of the race. Two of them were trying to fly, or rather they were flapping their wings and dancing about, pecking

38

at each other. Nature, the safest topic of conversation. Nature always had a calming effect.

"Fascinating birds," Mulder said, pointing to the quarrelsome ostriches.

With her eyes fixed on the rear-view mirror the neighbour seemed interested in little else than the occupants of the back seat, but a rapid glance to the side sufficed. "Oh, angry males. Those mannetjies will rip a man's stomach open if they're in the wrong mood, and they'll eat the heart too. They eat everything, even nails and tennis balls. One of them swallowed a kitten of mine once, and I could hear it mewing inside . . ."

Mulder gulped. "So what happened to the kitten?"

"What do you think? To a farmer those birds are valuable."

Mulder sat up, suddenly eager to know all about ostriches. Did they really stick their heads in the sand when danger loomed, and how many eggs did they . . . ? But the neighbour had long stopped listening. She was squirming in her seat, all her attention focused on the boy in the back.

"Just look at him," she murmured. "Have you seen his eyes?"

Mulder did not dare to look round. They drove into the hills, the view expanded. "It must be pretty wonderful growing up in a country like this."

"Not for everyone," she said bitterly. Not for her three sons . . . very bright, they were, Rhodes scholarships. There was no future for them in this country, unlike Australia. "They can't get good jobs here you know." She glanced at Mulder, hoping for a nod of sympathy. But he didn't notice in time, as he was twisting round to look at the boy, who was hunched over, sunk in pain. His eyes were narrow, his nose was slightly flat. Nice enough face, even if drained of colour, nothing like the tough kids in the under-village with their tattoos and missing front teeth.

The neighbour gestured towards the back and tapped her forehead. Her whole face was perspiring. She turned the air conditioning up another notch.

Mulder shivered. They were driving in a fridge.

The doctor shared his practice with a vet. It was unclear who had come for whom, but the parking lot was full. The neighbour wanted to drop her passengers as soon as possible, and pulled up by the entrance, warning-lights flashing. The maid helped the mother with the sick child into the building. The old woman said thank you in perfect English. The boy with the broken arm got out of the car without any trouble, but seemed unsure as to where he was. Mulder too made to get out of the car. The neighbour stopped him, saying they were going to the chemist. She had changed her mind – the chemist was better than the doctor. And he wouldn't be kept waiting there either.

She took a small mirror from her handbag, redid her lipstick and wiped off a fleck of mascara. Her hands were shaking. Sorry, she wasn't quite herself. It was because of that boy with the broken arm – he was a tikkop. A tik-head.

Mulder didn't understand.

"He's addicted to tik, crystal meth, a sort of super-speed. They smoke it or snort it, I'm not sure how it works." It was a gangster drug. Tik gnawed away at their brains. And affected their memories. Their emotions, too, and their conscience.

Mulder tried to calm her down. "We're not dead yet."

The neighbour gave him a look, shaking her head. "They'd murder their own mother."

*

A few minutes later Mulder was sitting with his trousers round his ankles in the small office at the back of the chemist's shop. An injection, some drawing ointment on the scabs, a bandage, and off he could go again. He was given a supply of antibiotics.

"Watch the alcohol," the chemist said with a wink.

The neighbour wanted to stop by at the supermarket. Mulder waited for her at the checkout. He felt too exhausted to do any shopping himself; he would be going somewhere with Donald tomorrow to stock up on tinned food. To kill time he read the free ads on the bulletin board: piano lessons, Zimbabweans looking for jobs, a housekeeper priding herself on her "obedience", offers of "babyseeting". There was one Sandra seeking "a good time". Beside Sandra hung Karen with "your body my hands!" Did the supermarket vet the content of the ads at all? His eye lingered on a yellowed card with a typed message from somebody looking for a pen friend on behalf of a 61-year-old male relative in prison, whose hobbies were reading, writing and politics; there was a P.O. box number, no name. Mulder removed the card from the board.

"Going to make a date?"

He spun round, startled. The neighbour stood behind him, smiling and clutching two full shopping bags to her chest.

"A mountain bike for sale," Mulder said coolly, glad to have thought of lying. "I reckon I could do with some exercise." He tucked the card into the back pocket of his trousers and relieved her of her shopping.

"How gallant you are," she said.

He offered to buy her a coffee. She drove to an outdoor café with a canvas awning. It was a tea room cum beauty parlour, all silk scarves, expensive handbags and make-up. Not a single dark face. A woman in a towelling turban waved from her chair: "Stienie!"

The neighbour excused herself and went over to her friend for "just a moment."

Mulder sat down at a table as distant from them as possible. Stienie . . . so *that* was her name! At last! He ordered water, opened the box of tablets from the chemist and read the information leaflet: kidney failure, cardiac arrhythmia, severe shortness of breath, rash. Just the ticket, he thought, bound to neutralise a rabid sausage dog. The stiffness was creeping up to his neck. Stienie was surrounded by chattering women.

"Sorry to keep you waiting," she said, turning up at his table after ten minutes. "They all wanted to see the pictures of my new grandchild."

Mulder drew up a chair for her, and dutifully subjected himself to admiring the baby photographs. Stienie stirred her latte. "Oh, if only I could cuddle him." But Kobus reckoned that Australia was too far. He didn't get on too well with her sons. Kobus was their stepfather.

"You could go on your own," Mulder said.

What, at the rate the rand was? No, it was too expensive. And anyway she couldn't leave her husband, he'd be at a complete loss, he couldn't even cook. Kobus went fishing, that was all he did these days . . . besides drinking.

Mulder nodded understandingly.

Stienie fumbled nervously for a tissue. She rested her plump hand on his for a moment. "No need to buy a mountain bike. We've got two in the garage. You can borrow one of ours."

*

Stienie wanted to take a different route home. "Not another car-load of misery, please." The maid wasn't a problem, Mulder wasn't to think that – she usually stayed behind with her relatives for the rest of the day.

"What about the sick child?"

"What can I do?" she sighed. "D'you reckon that's her only baba? She's probably got another two or three at home. From different fathers, too, often just kids themselves . . . I know a father aged thirteen. They all sleep with each other. Not that I care, but they don't use condoms. Single mothers get a little money from the government. Every cent is welcome, so they're all pregnant by the time they're sixteen. I wanted to help, you know, do something with my nursing diploma. Teach about hygiene and nutrition, show them how to give babies a bath, that sort of thing. But then I'd go back a week later to find the mother drunk again or high on drugs, and her baby in nappies that hadn't been changed for days. You can talk and talk, but they don't listen."

At a traffic light two youths jumped in front of the car waving sponges – windscreen-washers. Stienie honked angrily. "Sometimes it just gets to me, you know, all the begging, the resentment, the whining. Last year I couldn't take it anymore. I went to stay with my sister for a whole month."

The windscreen-washers melted away. Mulder made an apologetic gesture. A craven gesture, he judged afterwards.

"I expect you think I don't care, but that's what this country does to people."

Avoiding the high street, she headed towards a suburb and turned onto a track that would join the main road to the coast a few kilometres further on. The dust whirled. A pebble hit the rear window. Stienie slammed the brakes.

She laid her head on the steering wheel. "Do you mind if we turn back? Because I really ought to check up on that young mother. I wonder how her baba is, poor little thing. Maybe I'd better take them back with me after all."

The parking space at the doctor's and vet's clinic was still jammed with vehicles. As they inched past the entrance they caught sight of the mother and child. Stienie lowered the window. "What did the doctor say?"

"Pneumonia. We must go the hospital." The mother stared sullenly at the ground, fighting her distress, and hoisted the child higher up on her shoulder – it was drooling and the small head lolled back in the sun. Stienie clicked the doors open. "How could the doctor send her off like that? The hospital's up on a hill, half an hour's walk at least."

The mother climbed into the back seat with her child.

At the bottom of the hill they saw the boy with the broken arm, shuffling along the pavement. "Sent away, like her," Mulder said quietly. "Please pull over."

"Haven't we done enough?"

Mulder jerked the handbrake up. The engine shuddered and died. Stienie blared the horn.

The boy recoiled in fright, but his face relaxed when he saw Mulder coming towards him. He whimpered softly as he was led to the car. It took a hard knock on the window to get Stienie to unlock the back door. "Baie dankie," whispered the boy.

Stienie wondered aloud whether the boy had jumped the queue at the doctor's.

"That's what I'd have done. Pain isn't polite, you know."

She stared ahead, stonily. Mulder tried to catch her eye in the rear-view mirror. Had he gone too far? He wasn't sure why he was so set on doing this boy a good turn, but it was probably something to do with Stienie's fear. Her fear made him calm.

Mother and child were dropped off at the first aid post.

"Have you got money?" Stienie said.

"No, Mam."

A crackle of banknotes – a couple of hundred rand at least – for food and lodging, so the mother could stay with her child.

Mulder helped the boy out of the car. He could barely stand. The only bench in the hallway was occupied. Over the porter's lodge hung a saccharine picture of the Good Samaritan. Wheelchair? Assistance? No chance: it was the tea break. In the end Mulder lowered the boy onto a dehydrated indoor plant-box.

Stienie honked the horn.

Was it fair to leave the boy here to fend for himself? Empty-handed? The money was smoking in his wallet. He pulled out a few notes and handed them to the boy.

Stienie was waiting in the car park next to the first aid post. She was greatly relieved, there was no trace of her former irritation. She had heeded the voice of her conscience. And so had Mulder.

"You're a good person."

"No," he said. "I'm an egoist."

"You wanted to help, though, didn't you?"

"Yes, for my own sake. Means one less enemy."

That sounded too cynical, Stienie said.

Well, he could put it less crudely if she preferred: "Call it an impulse, the kind of human reaction that sets us apart from animals." He didn't mention that monkeys have empathy too. Even dolphins came to the rescue of their wounded fellows, as he had just read in an old newspaper. Mulder gave a little bark, in the dachs-hund's honour. He had that stupid dog to thank for becoming better acquainted with his neighbour.

Their mood grew increasingly confidential as they drove to the coast. Stienie's conscience was telling her she ought to divorce Kobus. By the time they drove up into the dunes Mulder knew more about his neighbour than was good for him. "Don't worry," he said, "I've got the memory of a tik-head."

It took him a while to find out which key belonged to his front door, and once in the hall there were all those other locks to sort out. Still, he was beginning to like his ramshackle home, especially when the sugar ants reappeared on the walls – a sure sign of rain, so he'd been told. There were dozens of them in the sink, not lugging food around, but quenching their thirst at the dripping tap. They were in transit, so to speak, having arrived in the early twentieth century with imported sugar from Argentina, and still seeking water, a ship to take them home.

Mulder opened a couple of windows to create a cross-draught and stepped into the bathroom to retrieve his laptop from the washing machine. He wanted to check his e-mails. He had no sooner switched on than he heard a scream. It came from across the road, a high-pitched, hysterical scream. He ran to the window and saw Stienie standing beside her car, hands up in the air.

He felt a ripple of panic: where were his keys? Hadn't he better hide his laptop first? But when he heard Stienie calling his name he left everything as it was and limped outside.

"*My handsak! My handsak!*"

Her bag had gone, stolen from the front seat while she was going back and forth taking her shopping into the house. She was crying. That fool Kobus, fokken, fokken Kobus still hadn't returned from his fishing expedition. She'd caught a glimpse of someone running away, a shadowy figure. Dark. Mulder wondered whether he was expected to give chase. Surely not with his bad leg?

The other neighbours from the top and bottom of the road came running, first the men, their wives close behind. Yes, they'd seen two boys, hoodlums from the under-village. They all trooped into Stienie's house. One of them rang the police, others busied themselves with blocking banking accounts and credit cards. Mulder wanted to console her: it was all his fault, and if there was anything he could do to help . . .

Stienie wasn't paying attention, she was too busy listing all the things in her bag: spare keys, mirror, lipstick, nail-file, make-up, driving licence, mobile . . . and, worst of all, the baby pictures, the pictures from Australia! What a shame! Three women put their arms about her, patted her shoulders, wiped away her smudged mascara.

The men stood around with their hands in their pockets waiting for the police. Could be hours before they arrived, there wasn't a police station nearby, not even in the under-village. Incredible, with all the crime about. The neighbour on the left knew what was required: a helicopter with a searchlight and machine gun. The neighbour from the top of the road returned home to collect his pistol, saying he'd let his ridgebacks out while he was about it – those dogs would attack a lion if need be. The skollies might be back, you never could tell.

Mulder promised to stop by the following day. These men don't like me, he thought. He had noticed their bull necks, and had been shocked by their display of temper. The stiffness was spreading to his jaw. His tongue was parched. Only a double whisky would help – at home, on his own sofa. Best possible antidote to stiffness.

Kobus returned at last, dropped off by a jeep full of noisy men with fishing rods. Mulder was lying on his sofa in front of the window, a second whisky to hand, listening out. Stienie had stopped wailing, there was no more swearing and shouting. The neighbours were still with her. Sundowner time. The doors to their patio were flung open and the lights switched on, the barbecue was lit, corks were popped. The hum of voices grew louder.

After his third whisky Mulder got up from the sofa. The smell of grilled meat had made him hungry. He decided to go the hotel, and pinch a roll of bog paper while he was about it. He took his small rucksack, switched on the outdoor security lights, and locked his front door. His hand shook. The moon lit up his path along the walls, but then a dog started barking, one of the ridgebacks from up the road. Lights flashed: burglar lights. Four men rushed out of the gate.

"Oh, it's him, the blerrie Hollander."

Kobus drew him in like a friend. "I hear you've been a great help to my wife." His breath smelled of cigarettes and wine, he was unsteady on his feet. Stienie welcomed Mulder with a kiss on the mouth. An Afrikaner custom, she explained. Mulder cringed. She had got over her fright, had even called her son in Sydney and woken up the whole family by mistake, and had heard her grandson's sleepy little voice calling her "Ouma". Granny: his first word of Afrikaans.

Kobus filled the glasses to the brim. "Wine makes you forget," he said. It was all very friendly. Yet more corks were popped. When the sparkling white wine ran out, bottles of red appeared on the table. The boerewors sausage was juicy and perfectly flavoured. The police had phoned to say they wouldn't be coming until the next day. Understaffed. It was a scandal, a fokken, fokken skande. It was always the same story – you did the best you could for them and they turned round and robbed you. Hardly surprising so many whites were leaving South Africa.

"Let's emigrate to Australia!" Stienie cried. "All of us!"

Everyone knew someone who had left the country for good. "There's a million of us living in London now," said the neighbour with the pistol outlined in the pocket of his shorts.

"We're staying put," Kobus said. Living down under was not for him: there was no better fishing in the world than at the Cape, and there was no way he would let a bunch of baboons make him leave.

There was a lull in the conversation. They all turned and looked at Mulder.

What did he think of all this, one of the women wondered. "It's not all bad here, you know."

"No, it's not," agreed the neighbour on the left. "We have a better life than most, mustn't forget that." There was the wind, the sea, nature . . . All things considered, it was a marvellous country, didn't he agree?

Mulder accepted yet another glass, his eight, or ninth. He had lost count. The wine had loosened his tongue, there was a trickle of sweat running from the nape of his neck down his back – the dachshund toxin was reacting.

"Yes, marvellous," Mulder echoed wholeheartedly. He became excited, and launched into Afrikaans – cod Afrikaans – to list its marvels: dancing ostriches, biltong, braais, delicious wines, best food, best game reserves, majestic landscapes.

Stienie beamed encouragingly. Kobus poured more wine, calling him boetie. "Yes, we're all boeties round here – mates, nice people!"

Mulder had to laugh, the drink was making him bolder. "Yes, it's a great country. I mean, where else do they blow your brains out for a mobile?" That was something he'd read in a newspaper.

What did he really know about the place? How much of the new, liberated South Africa had he actually seen?

Not enough. Still, he had spent many hours reading old Afrikaans newspapers. Partly on account of the language, the juicy expressions. As soon as you opened one you could feel the blood hitting you in the face. The blood of the dead student, stabbed nine times in a park in broad daylight for no apparent reason. The blood of thousands of rape victims, men as well as women. The bloodshed during the taxi wars. The blood of a heavily pregnant woman who was shot in the belly by a car thief and then went on to give birth to a crippled child. The cold blood of the corpses in the mortuaries that were carved up for use in morbid rituals. News that made the front pages shudder. The contaminated blood of the thousand Aids sufferers dying per day, whose bodies weren't even granted peace when buried because thieves were after the coffins. Wonderful, a place where they recycle coffins! And then the murderous political climate: nothing better than politics for getting rich quick by stealing and misleading and bribing court judges. A hospitable country, where people put up electrified fences and the broken glass glittered at you from the top of the wall. A land of opportunity, where a headmaster sells drugs to his students, half of whom risk falling into crime. Mulder recalled the tabloid story of the schoolgirl who fell into the clutches of a gang of youths on her way home and was raped repeatedly. When they finally let her go after a week the dazed girl went straight to a police station, where she was directed to a cell to calm down in and get some rest – but there was no rest for her, for that night she was sodomised by guards and policemen alike. Front page of the *Daily Sun*. Yessir, the *Daily Sun* sees everything!

"Problems in South Africa are real problems," Mulder said,

lapsing into Dutch. He was too drunk for any other than his mother tongue. Not a country to run away from, but to fight for. A free country, and yet the most dangerous place on earth. At least you felt alive, even if your life could be snatched from you from one day to the next.

The neighbours gaped at him. "Are you serious?"

"Never a dull moment." Was there ever any news about Holland in the newspaper?

Kobus yawned. The others looked down at their drinks, possibly deep in thought.

The neighbour on his right cleared his throat: "You've got a fair number of Muslims, though, haven't you?"

The ridgebacks growled. Could they hear somebody on the other side of the wall? The men leapt to their feet and ran to the gate. The pistol-toting neighbour narrowed his eyes, scanning the dune. Nobody in sight. No suspicious sounds. It could have been a baboon – a real one. Baboons came sniffing around the houses sometimes.

The sundowner was drawing to a close. The conversation flagged. Kobus wasn't used to staying up this late, Stienie began to sniffle. Mulder kissed her on the mouth.

Three neighbours helped him to hoist his rucksack and escorted him to his stoep. He could barely stand. None of the keys seemed to fit, but after fifteen minutes of concerted effort the front door creaked open.

He took a cold shower and, dripping wet, collapsed onto his bed. He pulled the sheet up over his face, the threadbare material enveloping him like a shroud. Outside, a shot rang out. Mulder could hear the blood throbbing in his brain, his heart pumping in a dizzying void, and he thought he saw stars on the ceiling – the Southern Cross.

A drop on his pillow. Another drop, like a shot, bang on his forehead. Mulder started awake, switched the light on and stared bleary-eyed at the circular stains overhead. There was a leak. Too groggy to shift his bed, he took his pillow and lay down on the sofa in the front room. The rain drummed on the window.

He woke up late in the morning, but the thunderstorm had not subsided. Dark swathes of cloud were rolling in from the sea. Donald had not turned up with his dogs. Mulder found a text message on his mobile: "*Sarah ill. Will call.*"

The air in the bedroom was tinged with damp and brine. The mattress was soaked through, and there was no warming sun in the sky. The circles on the ceiling had turned black, and the drops were now a steady trickle. One ceiling panel sagged. Mulder got up on a chair, raised the soggy board at one end and peered into a dark space. There was the sound of dripping on the attic floor. But where was the trapdoor? He went outside to take a look at the roof and then, standing in his bare feet, underpants and T-shirt, took a shower in the rain. The grass in front of his stoep was flooded and rivulets of sand swirled round his house. His thatched roof was a saggy hat. He stooped to pick up a handful of half-rotten straw.

"It's the baboons," a woman's voice said with a husky laugh.

He swung round to face a rain-drenched oyster-seller. "They like sliding down the roof."

Mulder looked up, open-mouthed.

"They come from the fields. Looking for food in the dustbins."

He gave an embarrassed smile and turned back to the house.

The woman shuffled after him: "Any oysters, mister?"

"No dankie."

"Oh, but you speak our language! You must be the new tenant from overseas." Her oysters came fresh from the rocks . . . the best of the coast.

"Another time, dankie," he said, shivering as he shut the front door in her face.

"Shall I come in and open a couple of oysters for you?"

Her basket scratched against the door.

She knocked a few times . . . might she shelter from the rain?

Mulder hesitated, cursed his prudishness and let her in. She kicked off her flip-flops and shook the water out of her long red skirt. He excused himself and went into the bathroom to change into dry clothes. When he returned the woman was bending over the basket, her breasts clearly defined under her wet blouse. "Here, this one's nice and plump," she said, holding out an open oyster.

He recoiled. No dankie, not before breakfast.

She slurped it up herself.

Mulder was sorry he had nothing to offer her: "Unless you'd like a slice of white bread and jam?"

She nodded towards the bottle of whisky on the table and sank down on the sofa.

Wasn't it a bit too early for a drink?

"Not for me, Meneer. I'm up a lot earlier than you."

He poured her a finger and sat down at the far end of the table.

They talked about oysters and where they were found and when they were at their tastiest. Her merchandise had a strong smell. Her name was Charmein. She said it slowly: "Char-mein. My Cape Town name." Yes, she'd lived there for years.

And now?

She jerked her thumb to the harbour. She had returned to her roots, her rotten dorp. For the sake of her child, a son who stole from her, a rotten son. Charmein emptied her glass in one go and held it out for a refill. He obliged, but asked no further questions, afraid she would never leave otherwise. Besides, he couldn't think of the right words. He quoted a garbled line from one of the poems Donald had told him to memorise.

Charmein burst out laughing: where had Meneer got that from? This couldn't be his first time in South Africa, obviously.

Well, it was his first visit since the liberation.

Liberation? Her eyes widened. "What d'you mean? What liberation?"

"I mean the liberation from apartheid."

Charmein pulled a face. "You don't really believe we've been liberated from apartheid, do you?" She fumbled in the pockets of her skirt and drew out a lighter and a crumpled packet of cigarettes. The tobacco was damp and the lighter took some time to produce a flame. Her skin lit up . . . brown, with dark lines. Handsome features.

"But in the old days . . ."

The old days? Beg pardon, surely Meneer knew the under-village? The dorp that was good enough for coloureds? Back then the street lights weren't all broken, back then it was safe for a woman to go about at night, back then there weren't any kids high on tik. Meneer should come and visit her some time, then he could see for himself how her people lived. Without proper sewerage. The government took no notice of their complaints. "We aren't black enough." And now the rainwater didn't drain away, so in this kind of weather half the village was flooded. She'd been a girl back then, but there was one thing she knew for sure: life was easier in the old days.

Mulder glanced furtively at his watch and slapped an ant off his wrist. "I must phone the estate agent, got to get somebody to fix my roof." He stood up.

She remained seated. Just as long as he didn't buy oysters off the young girls, she said. Or off the boys. Her cigarette had gone out, she rolled it between her lips, mockingly. She was sizing him up.

He held in his stomach.

She was curious about him: why wasn't he staying at his friend's house? Yes, she knew the Doctor . . . biggest house in the dunes – she'd been there once. "Doctor's a good man, yeah." Had he met the wife yet, Sarah? Oh, not yet? Sarah was French. And Meneer himself, was he married?

He said he had a headache.

She leaned back, flapping her skirt to dry it. A smell of oysters wafted towards him. One more drink then? Wouldn't he join her?

Mulder stood up. "Some other time perhaps." He dragged her basket to the hallway, leaving a dark stripe on the floor.

She went to the door, stepped into her slippers and hoisted the basket onto her hip with a sigh. "Surely not scared of an oyster, are you?"

He saw her out and waited until he heard her splash through the puddles, only then did he go back inside to draw the curtains. The front door refused to lock properly. He put a chair against the door, lay down on the sofa and inhaled her smell. Salty-sweet. The cushion was wet from her backside. Well, he'd been scared alright, not of a bad oyster, but of a desire he could not fulfil. He stroked his belly, then reached into his pants to adjust his sticky cock, that wilted appendage that had been hanging its head for years. Still, he had felt a twinge of arousal. Just a twinge.

He shuddered, thought of the old days, the accursed old days, and of his illicit adventures across the colour bar.

Mulder went to the hotel, the concrete box on the flat plain of no-man's-land. Until now he had given it a wide berth, because of its ugliness, and because of the manager being a racist in Donald's opinion. But why take any notice of the opinions of a friend who hadn't been in touch for the past two days? Save for a simple text message, just one word this time: *crisis*. The restaurant turned out to be quite reasonable: colonial Portuguese fare with lashings of piri piri on the fish and a waiter hovering at each table. And then there was the bar: seven different kinds of whisky. Which was as it should be in the only establishment for miles around with an official alcohol licence. A gathering of thirsty men: farmers from the hinterland, traders, a noisy cricket team and a couple of flashy young men with no discernible occupations. A lot of them had moustaches, and all of them were white.

They eyed him in silence as he came in. He made for a bar stool at the far end, sat himself down avoiding the stares, fiddled with a beer mat and ordered a whisky, a double J.&B. – Graham Greene's favourite. He reached over to pick a newspaper from a nearby table: *Die Burger*, a Cape daily. Good move: it showed he could read Afrikaans.

A man in a khaki hat two vacant stools further on slid another beer mat towards him. To break the ice Mulder mentioned a spectacular test match, with half an eye on the front page. "Did you see the match against Australia?" He read out the score, some names . . . Fine sport, cricket.

Khaki Hat nodded in agreement. Where did Meneer's accent come from? Holland! Did they play cricket there too?

"Not much, and not very well either. Holland could learn a thing or two from South Africa in that respect," Mulder said.

He was rewarded with a wide grin. The ice being broken, the rest joined in, plying him with questions: What did he think of South Africa? How did he like the Cape, the coast, the weather?

Everything was marvellous.

It was only after he ordered a round of drinks that he dared to ask whether the local fishermen also visited the bar.

Khaki Hat shifted his stool and looked at him suspiciously. "Why do you ask?"

Oh, no reason. Just wondering whether the fishing village had escaped flooding in the recent downpour.

"They're out at sea at this time of day."

"But there are so many boats on the slipway."

Wrong wind, probably, or else they were too drunk.

Wide grins all round.

Meneer was not to get the wrong idea, said an elderly Boer as he moved towards Mulder. Remarkable folk, the fishers. Quite extraordinary. But their culture was disappearing. You had to let the coloureds get on with their lives at their own pace. "Don't you agree, Karneels?" It sounded like an order.

Yes, Karneels the barman was ever in agreement. For professional reasons. He came from proud fishing stock and could tell Meneer everything he wanted to know about his people. But he was no sooner out through the swing doors for a bucket of ice than one of the cricketers, a man without a neck, nudged Mulder, saying: "It's all because of the quotas. One ton of lobster, five tons of cod, just one or two months of fishing and then they have to stop. Enough for a few families to live on, not a whole village." The neckless cricketer reeled off one scandal after another. All the money went to black politicians who had never fished in their lives, that much was clear.

"Drink is the only way to drown their sorrows," a second cricketer maintained.

"And tik," said a man in a polo shirt. Sure, tik was ruining the place. The trouble was the perlemoen. Was Meneer familiar with perlemoen? A shell, a protected species of mollusc. Also known as sea-ear, or abalone. Didn't he read the papers at all? Big business, very big. The main buyers were Chinese: perlemoen was an aphrodisiac.

The men sniggered at Mulder's ignorance. The stories came thick and fast: about the coastal waters, the unpredictable currents, the illegal catches. And about the young poachers risking their lives snorkelling along the coast at night to prise the shells from the rocks, about the booty being whisked off to secret stores in the hinterland by their accomplices, who would, likely as not, be attacked by gangsters. Half the payments at least were made in drugs. Hadn't he seen those brand-new dune buggies? Tik money. Yes, it was a canker. All along the coast, and in the under-village too. Tik was a time bomb. Everybody knew where the dealers lived. The police made raids, but nothing was ever found.

The men shook their heads and ordered more drinks. "All the police are corrupt," intoned a beer-belly at the other end of the bar, at which someone else jeered that there wasn't a uniform left you could trust these days. Jokes were bandied about. Mulder was barely able to follow it all. Soon they were reminiscing about "the bad old days".

Karneels rattled the ice in the bucket, long and hard. The talk died down; the men stared awkwardly into their glasses.

Khaki Hat broke the silence. Had Meneer kept dry alright in his little house up on the dune?

"No," Mulder said. "My roof's leaking, but how did you know where I'm living?"

They all knew where he lived. He was a friend of that guy Donald, wasn't he? (Khaki Hat articulated the name with emphasis.) Why wasn't he staying with him?

The entire cricket team pricked up their ears: Donald, yes of course, wasn't that the owner of the big house, the most valuable property of all, facing away from the village? Was he someone you could share a drink with? Strange, that: he never set foot in the bar. Too serious perhaps. What did Donald do all day anyway?

"He's retired." Mulder hesitated, he couldn't very well say it was none of their business. "But he still writes for medical journals. He's a scientist."

Bar stools scraped. Yes indeed, an egg-head. They grimaced. Did he know that his friend had tried to stop this hotel from being built? Imagine – the hotel, only the biggest employer around here! And he stoked the fishers up against the mayor, a coloured like them. He had been bombarded with letters and petitions. All perfectly typed. On posh notepaper, ha ha – and that when most of them were illiterate. It was all Doctor Donald's doing.

Mulder said nothing, thinking of his reason for being there in the first place: bog paper, something he had been without for days.

Outside, young girls were hanging around the visitors' cars

at the barrier of the parking lot. They wanted to go to town. Their buttocks bounced with impatience, one of them lifted her mini-skirt. It was a windless evening; the sea was holding its breath. Mulder waved his roll of toilet paper and ambled off towards the pier. A small boat without lights chugged into the distance. He heard voices on the hotel terrace, the bar was closing. Car doors slammed. Tyres squealed on the tarmac. By the time he turned back the parking lot was dark and deserted.

Cape Town, 1972. He had a delivery to make in the harbour, not far from Waterkantstraat, where the Taiwanese ships lay at anchor, plus the Norwegians and the Filipinos and the Greeks. They would stay for weeks on end. Colours mixed there in secret, foreign seamen with local women. Taxis crawled by, white chauffeurs in white dustcoats, with couples in the back. Marten was looking for The Manila, the dockside club where he was to deliver the envelope he carried stuffed under his shirt. The address wasn't right: people pointed him in different directions and not a single sailor had heard of it. He walked along a warehouse, where a black woman stood in the doorway.

"The Manila?"

The woman nodded, and he followed her down a long passage, past a white man in a cubicle, whom she greeted and who looked the other way as he pressed a button to unlock a metal door. They were alone, in a dark garage. Not The Manila. She pulled up her skirt. Somewhere overhead a car was started, they heard the crunch of rubber tyres on concrete – a car on its way to the exit. They ducked behind a pillar. Their legs got the full layer of light, after that they were in the dark again. He came. She peed in a corner, asked him for ten rand for the doorman and they walked outside in silence. It had taken five minutes. Five minutes which kept hammering in his brain. All night long.

The next day he was back, with the envelope as his passport.

"Hello, my friend."

Into the garage again. They did not move aside when a car circled downwards, they stood for a full second in the blazing headlights. She liked the light. No silence this time, no shame. Together they walked to The Manila.

The day after that she was waiting for him again; he paid the doorman in advance. Hush money, for being in violation of the Immorality Act. The bonnet they made love on was still warm. They kissed, and he thought: this is the life, I want to be with her forever. And she said, "You're a decent white man." A lie, but one he was happy to hear.

"You could rob me," he said.

"You could kill me," she said.

"Where are you from?" he said after their fifth encounter.

"Africa," she said.

"I love Africa."

"Oh everybody loves Africa. Give me a passport and I'm out of here."

In his imagination Mulder had long since explored the furthest reaches of the view from his window: the footpaths snaking to the hidden coves, the stretch of scrub which tore at your clothes, the low rocks where the currents were fraught with hazards, the tongue of land that emerged at low tide. He had leaped over rock pools with crabs and lobsters scuttling into the shadows, he had trampled beautiful shells underfoot. Quite the intrepid adventurer he was, in his mind.

Mulder lay back on the sofa reading *The Living Shores of Southern Africa*, the book he had helped himself to from the hotel lobby. He might yet return it, or he might not. The men at the bar had talked with so much enthusiasm about the coast that he needed to find out for himself what kind of creatures inhabited those waters.

The entry for perlemoen in *The Living Shores* was lavishly illustrated. Perlemoen was under threat from overfishing. The mollusc consisted almost exclusively of a mouth – suitable for grazing kelp, a sea bamboo which sometimes washed up on shore after a storm. The females also used it to ingest sperm, the male seed apparently floated in trails in the water, but only sexually mature females were interested, and then often only when eight years old or more. By that age most of them had already been ground up into powder to send to China, where abalone from the Cape enjoyed considerable fame as a stimulant. He held the photographs up to the light and peered at the row of holes in the shell. That was where the mollusc emptied its digestive system.

So now he knew.

And that was not all. The book took him into deeper waters, too, and he immersed himself in the effects of climate change, diminishing fish stocks and the need for quotas. All very worrying. He lay there for hours reading, another hundred and twenty pages to go and he would know all there was to know about the Cape coast. But what good would that do? How much of the coast had he actually seen? Up to now the new South Africa meant hiding behind high walls, diving for forbidden shells, womanising, kids snorting themselves out of their minds, and, closer to the bone, being bitten in the leg. So much for a rosy future.

Between chapters Mulder stared at the empty harbour, until he heard tapping on the window, a familiar sound by now: oyster-sellers. He no longer dismissed them summarily, as Donald and the neighbours had suggested he should, but did take the precaution of covering his laptop with a newspaper before letting them in. A sense of acute embarrassment meant he usually bought up their stock, only to tip the whole load into the sea at night when no-one was looking. He couldn't take the smell.

Charmein had called at least three times, in her steaming red skirt. He poured coffee for her, adding eight spoonfuls of sugar, and quizzed her about the village. Who lived in his house in the old days? When did the school burn down? But facts and figures were of no concern to Charmein: simply everything was different in the old days, the village was different, the sea was different – more fish in it. All the rest was too long ago, she had even forgotten when she had first been allowed to vote. Which year, which month? "The sun was shining." The weather was all she could remember (and even that only after Mulder pressed her). "Democracy isn't for the poor."

On her last visit they had sat together on the stoep, and he had waved cheerily at the neighbour from up the road, who drove past twice. On that occasion Charmein had drawn his attention to a hole in his sock, asking: "Who's going to mend that?"

"I'll do it myself," he lied.

Her fingernail tickled the bare skin above his sock. As soon as she left he stripped off his socks and threw them in the dustbin. There were to be no signs of weakness of any kind.

Children also jostled past his window now and then. He had taken the book outside a couple of times to show them the pictures of fish and ask if they were the same as the ones their fathers caught and what they were called in Afrikaans, but they just laughed. They had no patience with an old man's questions. To buy their trust he had made them peanut-butter sandwiches and offered them dried figs. But they didn't like brown bread, and later he had seen the figs lying discarded on the side of the road. Too wholesome, no doubt.

Yes, there was enough to eat in the house at last. Thanks to Donald, who had turned up unannounced in his car, apologising profusely about having neglected his friend – it had been a trying time, but Sarah was on the mend, thank goodness. Mulder would be meeting her the next day over breakfast, after their walk.

Donald had suggested driving to some farms to buy food directly from them, and to check out the roadside stalls in the hinterland. They had picked the best the region had to offer: ostrich biltong, wind-dried fruit, hard sweet rusks, mutton, chicken. (The freezer was purring contentedly.) "It won't be long now, and we'll be off on our trip."

The memory trip. Mulder wasn't sure he was looking forward to it. Even without getting up from the sofa more scenes came flooding back than he cared to revisit . . .

Catherine imposed herself, his great love from the old days, the woman who had introduced him to Fraternité. Suddenly she was there, in the crunch of the farmer's rusks he and Donald had bought en route, in the biltong and in the dried sour figs. She was there at the back of his throat, painfully so. Catherine had been his first introduction to South Africa. In Paris. If it hadn't been for her he'd have steered well clear of that tainted place, but she had persuaded him to undertake a forbidden journey to her native land – as an invisible outsider. She had committed him to a bitter struggle that was never really his. She did not take to the barricades in person, but threw her money into the fight, a lot of money. She supported political refugees and had a fine nose for young men who might blossom in Fraternité. Donald had been recruited by her, a few years before Marten. But she was discretion itself, studying art history at the Sorbonne. Her father was a South African winegrower, a descendant of prominent Huguenots. She was ashamed of her country. She was ashamed of her father's wealth. And she couldn't get by without it.

Their love was secret. ("No affairs between freedom fighters!") It was especially important that Donald, who was responsible for Mulder's instruction, should be kept in the dark. But when Mulder was in South Africa as Marten he was lonely and scared, and couldn't resist writing her passionate letters. Risky, but that was part of the attraction. His ardour was not without effect. Catherine packed her suitcase with the false bottom and flew into his arms. In complete secrecy! They were together for only a week, one week without fear, without lookers-on. They explored the vastness and ate of the land, like French gourmets on honeymoon – sour-fig jam, biltong and sweet Ouma Rusks. It was a game, but he loved her more than ever. Their love made him pure again.

So now he was back in the Cape, to plug the gaps in his memory. He reread the lilac letter he had found along with several others in a drawer before he left home. It was the best letter of the batch. And the most painful. Sender: Catherine. Stuffed into his suitcase at the last minute so as to have her close to him on this South African journey too . . . *"My darling bad boy, you're in all the papers! I knew it was you straight away from the description: tall, curly hair, northern accent. How daring of you!"* Lines of appreciation for his theft of the medieval manuscript (tens of thousands of francs!), but alas, no use to him for convincing Donald of the accuracy of his account of his crime in the *Bibliothèque Nationale*. Too personal.

Mulder could dream her letter . . .

Tu te plains de mon absence . . . You complain of my being gone, you say that after spending a few wonderful nights together I am sometimes unreachable for days and that I disappear too frequently from your life. But my love refuses to be tied down. I am married to freedom. Let us give our friendship some space, or it will shrink away. I despise man-made boundaries. Boundaries of colour, language, land. From an early age I always looked up to people who took no notice of those boundaries, like the grape-picker who passed for a cousin of our cook. I was about sixteen when I first came across him. I had never been in the servants' quarters before, a row of huts at the foot of the hill. My father forbade me to go there. But I had spotted that particular picker at work, he was uncommonly black for the region, he stared at me quite brazenly. One afternoon I followed him. For me, apartheid was already on the wane. The grape-picker showed me where he lived, a shabby little room without windows or electricity; he used to read by candlelight. A cliché. And for the rest too he lived up to expectations: he wanted to continue his education, but had no money. He stole from the cook and he stole from me, or rather, I let him help himself. He had been looking for work and broke the law against so-called Bantus living on white land. But he was unpredictable, too: when we were found out he asked my father for my hand in marriage. He was bundled into in a police jeep and I was sent to Paris to cool off. He was a tender lover. His brazenness was exhilarating. He was the beginning. The first boundary I crossed.

The letter shook in Mulder's hands. He could hear her voice in the words, just as when he first read them, but now he listened differently. Then it had sounded like a thrilling pact: independence first and foremost. And now? Now, the grape-picker cried out – her liberating lover. Had her lips liberated him too?

"You'll see springbokkies, kelp gulls, boubou shrikes, fish eagles, and even Damara terns – if you're lucky, because they're very rare. And who knows, we may spot one of those stinky legless lizards."

Donald walked with his head bowed, scanning the ground for animal tracks. He showed Mulder the tunnel of a striped grass-mouse, the sinuous trail of a snake. And there in the sand, did he see that string of claw prints and bumps with lines down the side? Just as if a tumbleweed on legs had come bowling past. Donald got down on his knees and sniffed: "Porcupine."

"How come you know all these things?"

"It's my Hotnots blood," Donald said wryly.

The two friends had crawled under a wire fence and were now walking along the dusty paths of a nature reserve. Without the dogs. Sarah had kept them at home. "She doesn't feel safe without them," Donald said. "She's having a hard time." He didn't go into details. "Happens now and then. Sorry to bother you with this."

Just as well, though, that now he had the chance to show Mulder the surroundings at leisure, so soon after the rains. Tender grasses had shot up, white and pink flowers, buds smelling of honey – nectar for the bokkies. Donald pointed to a patch of disturbed soil. "Look, they've been dancing on the dune."

At an intersection of winding paths Mulder spotted a different sign in the landscape: freshly turned-up sand, troughs along battered vegetation. A Land Rover?

"Kak." Donald stamped his foot. "Kak, kak." A buggy, obviously. What were they after in this wilderness? Poachers? Yes, but how did they get in with their buggies? The park was fenced off all around.

"Perlemoen can buy you anything," Mulder said. "Including access to restricted areas."

"You're well-informed."

"I keep my ear to the ground too, you know."

"I thought I was supposed to be your guide." Donald stared gloomily at the wheel tracks. "You'll hear too much and see too much for your own good if you're not careful." He adjusted the focus of his binoculars and studied the horizon. There! There! A cloud of dust was drifting out to sea. Donald ducked behind a shrub, pulling Mulder after him. "They mustn't see we've come without the dogs."

Mulder's leg was hurting. "Let's go back."

Donald wanted to go after them. "I'm collecting evidence."

"Playing the detective, are you?"

"No, but the man those poachers work for is the mayor's brother, the number one drug dealer around here. And the mayor turns a blind eye, needless to say."

Donald turned the buckle of his belt inwards so it wouldn't catch on anything, and crawled towards the ridge of thrown-up sand. Mulder held back, but then he too turned the buckle of his belt inwards, as though he had no choice. Their shoulders touched. They had been in this situation before, drenched in sweat and hiding behind bushes, but that was when they were practising la filature in the Bois de Boulogne. Lessons in shadowing – now

71

with mud-bespattered faces, now in a suit and tie behind a news-paper. They had shadowed and spied together countless times. Not only did Donald know all about politics, he was also a first-rate commando. That was how they had got to know each other really well, on the practical level rather than the abstract. They were stuck with each other, chosen as a team by the Chief: the pupil and the mentor, Marten the politically naïve romantic, Donald the ideol-ogist. Worlds apart, but they found each other in the shared banned language and boyish sense of adventure.

A smile, a wink, a mocking glance and Mulder followed Donald along the offending wheel track towards the sea. Two super-annuated Boy Scouts. A hint of the old comradeship came back to them as they made their way, bent double over flat stretches where the sound of the surf carried far, crawling over the dune-tops, and upright again in the valleys, where it was so quiet that Mulder could hear his own heart beating.

They came to the first cove. Donald blew the sand off his binoc-ulars and described what he could see: pristine strand and a glisten-ing sea thick with plankton. The poachers' tracks disappeared for a moment, but at the top of the next dune they caught sight of them again snaking round to the following cove. Half a mile further on they saw two dune buggies hidden in the bushes (the engines were still warm), from where a freshly trodden path led down to a secluded inlet with spurs of rock and crescents of sand.

The shore offered no cover, so they crept around the rocks. Black-back gulls circled overhead, their beaks wide open. Every shadow resembled that of a man. On the last stretch of sand, beyond an overhang of rock, lay a boat wreck, half on its side in the seaweed. Donald passed the binoculars to Mulder. The name of the boat was faintly legible: *Baby Prudence*. The deck, wheelhouse and portholes were thickly encrusted with rust. A lobster boat, according to Donald. How long had it been there? They inched their way forward. Donald took pictures with his mobile.

"Modern man," Mulder said.

"Quiet!"

Music . . . was that music they could hear? Above the roar of the surf? Donald grabbed the binoculars. "There are people in that wreck." But he couldn't see anything. They heard an engine . . . A rubber dinghy had entered the bay and was now speeding along the rocky shore. Water police, patrolling the coastline. Mulder and Donald lay low. The roar of the engine died away.

The sound of the sea took over again. They couldn't hear any music. No sign of any movement on board. Donald wanted to stand up and take a closer look, but Mulder pulled him down just in time. He pointed to a head rising from the deck hatch – someone was clambering out. It was a man, then another man, both burly types. They helped a woman over the high surround. She had difficulty walking. After her came two girls, very young, school age by the look of them. Finally a boy with his arm in plaster. Donald's mouth fell open.

"I know that kid. He's from the village," he said.

Mulder kept silent.

They held their hands and faces under the garden tap and walked across the terraces of Donald's house, which was large, white and stark. Fabulous view of the sea, private flight of stairs down to the beach. A dune enclosed by high walls, with its back to the harbour and the neighbours. The kitchen windows were wide open. Sarah, with a tea towel wrapped round her head, was stirring a saucepan. Mealiepap. She enunciated the word with revulsion. Traditional maize porridge for Donald and his friend from overseas. Mulder shook hands with her over the steaming cooker.

"Where have you been?" She picked a bit of straw from Donald's hair. "Did you get to see the dolphins?"

"No," he said gruffly. "We had other things on our mind." He threw Mulder a towel and studied the photographs on his mobile phone.

"Ah, *politique*, I suppose," Sarah said. Her English sounded like a plaintive sort of French. "Pity about the dolphins. There were at least twenty of them coming past! Less than an hour ago, right here, below the terrace." And springboks – surely they had seen some bokkies?

Donald had no patience for discussing Nature, not just now! He had to phone the mayor at once, this minute, and he strode angrily to his study.

"But the omelette: you said you were going to make the omelette!" Sarah lifted the porridge pan off the cooker and untied the tea towel from her head. She went to an antique sideboard and took out two soup bowls. For the porridge. She wore a tight black dress and a velvet Alice band in her brown hair.

Mulder helped to lay the table.

"Donald gets so worked up about his village. Hasn't had time for anything else the last couple of days. People coming to the gate all the time. There's a crisis." Her soles crunched on the floor-tiles – sand, brought inside by hurried, unwiped shoes. The dogs were asleep in a corner.

Mulder looked at her legs. Patent leather shoes with a little bow.

"Do you do much walking here?"

"That depends on the dogs," she said. "It's not safe for a woman to go off on her own in the dunes."

Donald entered the kitchen, fuming. "They're crazy, completely fokken crazy. I report a drugs den and the mayor lectures me about trespassing. The village is going to the dogs. All the kids are going to the dogs." He poured himself a cup of coffee. "We must have some kind of meeting. Council of elders, or whatever's left of it. The travelling pastor, for all I care." He leafed through his address book.

Sarah held out the frying pan. "Shall I make the omelette, then?"

Donald was not listening. He would get in touch with a journalist – oh yes, he still had his contacts, see what he could come up with. And he knew a government minister, a pompous ass, but status helped. The wreck, the mayor . . . the whole story needed to be told. Donald ranted on in broad Afrikaans. Hendrik had been seen in the village again, with the wrong friends. Skollies with too much money in their pockets. Who was Hendrik? Mulder ventured to ask.

"The boy with the broken arm. I help his mother."

Sarah set the pan on the table: porridge with a skin on it.

Donald nudged Mulder, hissing, still in Afrikaans, "You'd better keep this in mind, for your own good: you know nothing, fokken nothing, so you just keep your mouth shut, O.K.?"

"*Arrête!*" Sarah cried. "*Arrête!*" The dogs flattened their ears and moved closer together. "Stop this Afrikaans! Speak English, *ou Français*." She spun round to leave the kitchen, but Donald grabbed her by the arm.

Mulder felt in the way. "I'm sorry."

"She understands Afrikaans perfectly well," Donald said, thumbing a text message on his mobile.

"*Parlez-vous Afrikaans?*" Mulder asked.

"A little." She looked away at the dogs.

"She can even swear at you in Afrikaans," Donald said without looking up. He clattered a ladle of mealiepap on his plate. "But when I speak Afrikaans it gives her a headache. Migraine."

Sarah sank onto a chair and Donald scoffed down his porridge. Mulder praised the sausage: "*Un bon saucisson sec.*"

Sarah nodded absently, and from then on addressed only the dogs, in whispered French.

Donald apologised in the hallway. "I was a bit harsh." He pushed the front door open and the sun struck them in the face. "Perhaps I just get too involved, but there's so much that needs getting done here." Mulder gave him a glassy look. They strolled towards the garden gate, lingering in the shade of the high wall.

"I can't wait to go on that trip of ours. But, er, please bear with me, I'm not sure how long I can keep Sarah here. She needs to get away from time to time."

76

"I hope I'm not being any sort of nuisance."

"No, don't worry. Ever since we came to live here fifteen years ago she's spent half the time in France. Her coming and going like that has saved our marriage."

They heard voices out in the road. Catcalls. The scratch of nail-sticks and footsteps running away. Someone knocked on the gate. "What now?" sighed Donald. It was a woman, a girl rather, with a toddler in tow and a baby on her arm. She nodded towards Sarah's car, which was parked in front of the garage door. The tyres had been slashed.

Donald went over to inspect the damage, saying nothing.

The woman trailed after him – would the Doctor give her ten rand, please.

"Later, later, come back after ten." He patted the toddler on the head and hurried back to join Mulder at the gate. "You mustn't let them get the better of you," he said. "Sometimes you need to put your foot down."

There were baboons cavorting on the thatched roof; tufts of straw dropped onto the stoep. Mulder was sitting at his table checking his e-mails, and couldn't be bothered to chase them away. Kindness to animals was a virtue, after all. Only when he heard the back gate rattle did he get up to take a look. There were two baboons sitting rump to rump on top of the wall, their tails curling around each other. The one on the right stroked the one on the left and gave a little pat, after which the left one returned the gesture. Then the tails became entwined again. Stroke and curl, stroke and curl. Below-the-belt pantomime, but no less poetic for that. "Be kind," was what those tails were saying, "and you'll never be alone."

The shadows lengthened, rumps were shifted in search of warmer stone. And up swooped the tails: two warm, living paintbrushes against the wall. Caressing followed by crapping. Then two cinnamon-tinted curls in an embrace.

Mulder saw the quivering hairs on the tips of their tails, and hugged himself a little too.

There was a man on the stoep. He wore an airman's cap with ear-flaps. "Any trimming?"

"What do you mean?" Mulder said.

The man held up an electric hedge trimmer. "Verges, dune grass, bush. Thirty metres extension lead."

"Thirty metres!"

"I'm quiet, and I reach far."

Mulder excused himself. "It's not my property, you should go and see the estate agent."

Ah, Meneer was new here, was he? Trimmer-man could tell by the accent. He came from Transvaal himself, from the high veld. Hitched a ride in a refrigeration truck. He sniffed at his shirt sleeve. Fish, frozen fish. Saw the sea for the first time in his life this morning, at daybreak. It was just like they said, only wetter. What a waste! Where did all that water come from? And those waves! "I may be smelly, but I'm not going in there, too noisy." He pointed to the plugs in his ears. "I hear too much."

"It's the wind," Mulder said.

No, he meant that he heard quiet sounds. Snakes, leeches, eyes.

"Eyes?"

Trimmer-man gave Mulder a questioning look. His skin was

peeling, his lips were chapped, like dried clay. Could Meneer spare him a glass of water?

Mulder turned to go to the kitchen. The man followed him. Too late to send him away, so they might as well have some tea and a farmer's rusk.

The man yawned over his cup of tea. Oh yes, he'd had a rough night. The parking lot opposite the hotel was a very busy place, very noisy, a lot of fighting and shouting. "Blind-drunk kaffirs."

Where did he normally spend the night?

Cars, sheds, barracks.

"There aren't any barracks around here and the only shed is a cold store," Mulder said, brushing some crumbs and flakes off the tabletop.

What about those posh houses, wasn't there some sort of army general living over there?

"Not that I know of."

A politico maybe? Well, he'd had his fill of them, big-mouths with bags of money, the liars who'd made him fight for his country, right up to Angola, and who'd given it all away to the terrorists he'd fought against in the first place. Just like that. *Ratatatat.* Trimmer-man fired an imaginary round of ammo, with his mouth full, spraying Mulder with crumbs. Three comrades, *ratatatat*, three of his best mates mown down before his very eyes. Blown to bits. Not a scratch on him though, only thing was he now suffered from dizzy spells, and couldn't take the sun. First a war hero, now a criminal. If he ever ran into his colonel, or any other of those traitors like Botha or de Klerk, he'd string them up with his thirty metres of extension lead. Revenge had a long arm.

Mulder splashed his face with water from the kitchen tap.

Trimmer-man lit a cigarette.

Mulder looked at his watch.

Trimmer-man picked up his electric tool and made for the door. "When I came back from the war I didn't have a belt, no shoelaces either. They were afraid I'd do myself an injury. My little girl thought I'd joined a circus. It made her skip with pleasure. So now I go around with thirty metres of extension lead. I am alive and I believe in God. It's the fish I'm scared of."

The crack of gunfire came back to him, the force of the kick, the smell of cordite in the woods near Saint-Cloud. Lessons in marksmanship from Donald and Catherine. The pistol, a brand-new Beretta from Italy, had been provided by her. It was all about being able to handle a weapon. (There was no mention of using it to threaten or kill.) When scarcely out of boyhood, a South African would sooner learn to shoot than to drive, and there was every chance Marten would have some such item foisted on him during his mission. To complete the picture he would spend a couple of months as a student at Stellenbosch University, the spawning ground of the Afrikaner establishment, but to avoid arousing suspicion he had to live outside the campus, in a politically non-sensitive environment. Catherine had arranged a room for him in a boarding house not far from the barracks, a transit home for soldiers on leave. He was to start by making a good impression there. Shooting at tin cans after a braai, writing his name in bullet holes on a plank – soldiers' rituals.

Marten was to steer clear of political debates at the university, in so far as they occurred at all. The security police were everywhere. He was to have no opinions, for Marten was just another student from overseas, friendly and intent on building bridges between two languages and two peoples, the Afrikaners and the Dutch. He had been selected by Fraternité for the colour of his skin and the sound of his native language, and also for his political naïvety – the instruction leaflet of a stain-removal spray being of more interest to him than a treatise on Marx. He was to mix with other students without arousing suspicion, and to make contacts as the occasion arose, casually, particularly among young intellectuals with a desire for change. There were many who wanted change, but they didn't know how to go about achieving it. For critical Afrikaners in those days it was nigh impossible to escape from their clan. Rebellious political leaders were in prison or in exile, only insiders knew the way to the underground resistance. Each colour-coded community was crowded in on itself, with relations between the various ethnic groups being virtually non-existent. It was up to the innocent European student, the young man with his smart cufflinks and signature brogues, to gauge the mood and pass on the names of potential sympathisers.

Interest in firing guns was a camouflage, as was his appearance.

Marten was a quick learner when it came to loading the pistol, pulling the trigger smoothly and not screwing up his eyes like a girl at the last moment. Donald kept repeating his mantra: Direction, Dedication and something else beginning with a D (Discretion? Defiance? Devotion?). Three serious D's, anyway. Hitting a target was child's play to Catherine, who would shoot a pine cone off the branch of a tree and then sniff the barrel in triumph. Laughing, as ever.

She showed him how to take aim, she massaged his shoulders, uncurled his cramped fingers. Hip against hip. He had felt a frisson at the time. She smelled so wonderfully of nothing. And Mulder felt a frisson again now, thinking of her, of how her dress billowed in the wind, how she stroked the hairs on his forearm with the

Beretta. Teasing, provoking. For fun. Had it all been fun to her?

Donald droned on: Direction, Dedication, D . . . He scratched a letter M on the bark of a felled beech tree, took thirty steps back and fired. Marten failed to hit the carved initial. Another shot, yet another, and more. Hardly a recognisable letter. Time for a new trunk, a clean slate.

He shot a C with five bullets. He was thrilled and went on to shoot a heart-shape. Twelve bullets. The Beretta felt red hot in his hand. Catherine applauded enthusiastically. Donald stamped his foot.

Mulder was shocked by the memory. The whole idea of shooting had excited him . . . the skin of polished steel. Could there be a murderer lurking inside him? Did he take after his father after all, the army man whose influence he tried to avoid in every respect? Whose medals he had been made to kiss as a boy? He had never wanted to be like him. Regimental, addicted to giving orders. Mulder despised men who needed a gun to assert their virility, and yet the crack of the first few shots had brought on an erection.

"Well, they'll have to manage with that as best they can." Donald stretched and looked at his computer screen with satisfaction. He had drafted an official missive to the local council, reporting the presence within the municipality of a boat wreck that was being used as a drug den. School-age children had been sighted there, and smugglers. He had photographs to prove it. So all that remained now was for his statement to be read by the councillors – assuming they were sufficiently literate. There was no point in expecting a response from the mayor, who had a horror of words of more than three syllables. Dealing with the post was something he left to his subordinates.

Mulder poured coffee and stared at the screen. The dogs lay beside the fireplace; it had been raining since early morning. By now Sarah had presumably arrived at her sister's flat in Paris. She had taken the plane the previous evening, driving to the airport in her car with the brand-new replacement tyres. She had decided to go away on the spur of the moment it seemed, but after she had left, Donald discovered that the fridge was over-stocked, as were the freezer and the larder. "I won't need to do any shopping for the next month or so," he said. She had left a note for Mulder, apologising for her sudden departure and asking him to keep an eye on his friend.

There was no more talk of taking trips. Donald had too much on his mind. Even the morning walk had been too much for him, so that after a quick tour of the dune they had turned back. Donald had gone straight to his study, the untidiest room in the house, but insisted they have breakfast together at his desk. Between mouthfuls of lumpy porridge he sorted the post, intoning the senders' names without once looking at his guest.

Mulder wasn't paying attention; he was reading the spines in the bookcase. Walls covered in politics and history and, in pride of place, beneath a label saying "Pornography", a row of novels that had been banned by the old regime.

Donald's bookcase in Paris had sported an identical label. In fact the study as a whole was a replica of the room he had occupied in Paris, complete with a sagging sofa and a noticeboard cluttered with old newspaper photos of international resistance and rebellion. Nowadays it was the village taking up all his time and energy. He had got in touch with a reporter at *Die Burger*. It was about time people knew about the problems in the fishing community and the corruptness of the mayor. He had already sent off the photographs of the wreck.

"That's brave of you," Mulder said.

"Pointless, you mean." Donald downed his mug of coffee and slid a fat envelope over to Mulder. Appeals and queries from fishermen. Scrawled notes, often no more than a few lines on a piece of brown wrapping paper. Doctor please do this, Doctor please do that.

Mulder skimmed through them: "How deferential they sound."

"That hasn't changed. Whites of any standing are still called Doctor. Meneer Doctor, preferably." No, they didn't bother him with their ailments, and he had never held a surgery in the village,

85

though sometimes he couldn't resist distributing medicines. The fishing folk needed his help in dealing with the new South African bureaucracy, spelling out the small print. The majority of the boat owners could barely read or write, their principal means of communication being the mobile phone. They had difficulty understanding the workings of the quotas, some didn't even know what the word meant. ("Meneer Quota – where does he live?")

Donald encouraged the fishing community to stand up for their rights, and with success, for it rained appeals, especially from women on behalf of their husbands. The Doctor's letterbox overflowed. He had become a sort of general adviser to the under-village . . . Why were some families obliged to have their catch weighed and not others? Was the Doctor aware that poachers were constantly being given preferential treatment? Did he know that tik was being handed out for free in the school yard?

Donald flung open a drawer. "Here! Found in my letterbox last week: sewage-disposal tax. In the name of progress. Would I please fill out the forms. I'm not their clerk, for Chrissake. They haven't even got a sewage system! No drainage either, they've got fokken nothing. Return to sender, I say, with a big fat cross on the envelope. Sewage pipes in place first, then payment."

Mulder frowned as he inspected the forms. "Do you know what you're letting yourself in for?"

Donald shrugged. He had his letter to the council to finish, for which he needed a forceful ending, something that would make them sit up and take notice. Mulder, pleased to have been taken into his friend's confidence, suggested various alternative turns of phrase, none of which were deemed satisfactory.

"*Jullie vermoor ons dorp!* You are murdering our village! how does that sound?"

"How many slashed tyres do you think your letter is worth?"

"But something has to be done! Tik, tik tik, wherever you go. The magic powder's all over the place, and anyone who doesn't join in is a wimp. Over half the kids in the village are addicted." Donald began to list them: "There's Senekal, son of Saartjie, thirteen years old, Edith Erasmus the preacher's daughter, fifteen. And Japtha, and Heinz who's had a stroke and he's not even twenty." He leafed through the letters from parents asking for help. Tik was destroying entire families. But what could he do? One of the names made him swear aloud. Hendrik! The boy they'd seen emerging from the wreck on the beach! Hendrik with his arm in plaster. A tik-head, like the rest.

"What's so special about him?" Mulder said.

"He's the brightest one of the lot, damn it! And the most imaginative. The village needs boys like him. In the summer he puts on fancy dress and goes to the beach to scrounge magazines from tourists. He's crazy about the pictures." Donald had secretly paid the boy's school fees, although there was little for him to learn in the village. He was too old, anyway – over fifteen – but his mother had no money for schooling elsewhere, let alone for travelling expenses. After a lot of bother Donald had managed to secure him a grant and a place in a boarding house in town. Hendrik was to pursue his education in Distriksdorp. Not surprisingly, the news had met with a fair amount of jealousy, as well as indignation: why was that rogue being rewarded? "Hendrik is the son of a prostitute."

"Not so exceptional, surely."

"It is if your mother has no shame and your father's a Chinese seaman." Hendrik was an outsider. His eyes were too slanted. And bastards wanted to belong as much as anybody else. Certainly, he was vulnerable, not that he realised it himself, and now he was snorting his brains to a pulp. How could he have slipped from Donald's grasp?

A helicopter flew over, which set the dogs off barking and tearing around the house. Mulder went over to the window. "Ah, visitors! The police. Just what you wanted."

Donald barely looked up. "That would make the headlines," he said.

Mulder had to shout to make himself heard: "Shall I go and take a look?"

"Don't even think of it. Before you know it bullets will be whizzing round your ears."

The rain had slackened, there were gulls shivering on the terrace, huddled up against the gusty wind. Mulder opened the terrace door, lifted his face to the tepid raindrops, but the helicopter had already passed from view. He saw scudding clouds beyond the broken glass on top of the wall. How can people live this way? he thought. So cut off. How can you save a village you banish from your sight?

Not even from the far end of the terraces and the fenced-off steps down to the beach was there anything to be seen of the village. A megaphone could be heard crackling unintelligible orders, children whooped, and in the distance buggies raced across the dunes. Mulder went back inside.

"I don't know about you," he said, "but I'm going for a leg stretch."

Donald came out from behind his desk. "Leave those people alone, they feel humiliated enough as it is," he grumbled. "They can do without some white foreigner sticking his nose in."

"Why is my being white such a big deal? What makes them so

88

touchy anyway? I want to form my own opinion. You don't meant to say the village is off-limits, do you? Because I could do with some mental exercise."

The bell rang out, loudly and persistently.

The dogs bounded to the gate, a husky voice sounded on the terrace, distraught, tearful. Donald ran to the front door. Flip-flops slapped down the corridor. Donald instructed Mulder to stay in the kitchen and keep an eye out for intruders. "The gate doesn't lock properly."

The caller wore a white headscarf and was quickly ushered into the study. Mulder didn't get a chance to see her face, and had to force himself not to go and listen at the door. That voice, that briny, salty, oyster smell . . . He took a step forward, tilted his head, straining to catch a name, a clue, but Donald had switched the radio on – the old trick to foil eavesdroppers.

The kitchen was a shambles. Mulder filled the dishwasher, made coffee, and wiped down the draining board. Moving a plate of fresh cactus fruits, he got his fingers covered in tiny spines. He rinsed his hands under the tap but only managed to rub the brown tufts deeper into his skin. Tweezers, that's what he needed, where could he find a pair of tweezers? He hunted in drawers and cupboards. He had no idea where the bathroom was in the big, spooky house, and slunk down a long corridor, opening one door after another.

The dogs were barking again: the sound of footsteps on the terrace. Mulder banged a few doors.

"Quiet!" Donald shouted from his study.

Someone had slipped into the kitchen. Mulder braced himself. With leaden feet he approached the figure in white overalls. "What do you want?" he asked gruffly.

The response was a broad, disarming grin. It was Winston, the house-painter. As old as the hills and bent like a fishhook. He had the key, he said, and had come to fix the lock on the gate.

So soon?

He happened to be passing.

Mulder rubbed his hand nervously. Ah, prickly pear – Winston recognised the culprit at once.

"Do you have tweezers?" Mulder said.

No, Winston had a better idea: there was an aloe growing by the gate. He went outside and returned with a long fleshy leaf oozing moisture. Aloe was soothing – smear the pulp on the affected skin and the spines would come out of their own accord.

Sure enough, the painful itching stopped almost at once. But Winston was not minded to leave. He hung around the sink for a while and then settled himself at the kitchen table. Sprawled against the back of the chair, legs flung wide, head barely reaching above the table, he kept his eyes fixed on the corridor. The radio in the study was playing sad music.

Mulder poured two large mugs of coffee.

Wouldn't the Doctor be wanting coffee as well, Winston mused, or was he still busy with "that woman"?

Mulder shrugged. Better not disturb them. Winston shook his head dolefully. Yes, trouble in the dorp again, big trouble. The police were searching all the houses from top to bottom.

"A guest at the hotel has been robbed."

All that fuss for a hotel theft?

"Must have been some big shot – everybody's talking about it." Why did Meneer think the woman had come to see the Doctor? Old Winston had his eyes about him, for sure, he'd just seen her leave the hotel, not for the first time, and he'd seen her go to the

Doctor's house in tears, not for the first time either. The Doctor ought to be careful. People gossiped. Just as well Madame Doctor wasn't here.

Winston shook his head knowingly. The house was empty, and it was too big, a man would want company from time to time, which was why he was keeping an eye on the Doctor. The Doctor couldn't look after himself properly. He'd known small-baas for such a long time, knew him almost as well as the house. Yes, old Winston knew every stone, he'd helped to build it . . . did Meneer know . . . Winston rambled on and on.

Mulder was only half listening, his ear kept being drawn to the door of the study. Was that sobbing he could hear now, or was it the radio?

The sun came out, casting shafts of light across the corridor. From the study came the sound of chairs scraping over floor tiles. The doorknob moved. Winston bolted. Mulder wanted to stand up too, but Donald and the woman were already on their way to the front door. She was sniffling, her headscarf had come loose and she wore a red skirt. Mulder couldn't see her face properly against the backlight. "Charmein?"

She pocketed her handkerchief and gave a wan smile.

Donald bundled her outside. No sooner had the gate clanged shut than he doubled back to Mulder. "How come you know her?"

"So? I talk to people sometimes, you know."

"Don't tell me, I know what you're like with women. Keep away from her, for goodness sake. She's having a rough time. Very rough." Donald was visibly edgy. "Charmein is Hendrik's mother."

Mulder gulped "Nice woman, she's come to my door a couple of times. No idea she was a whore, but that doesn't mean I shouldn't talk to her, does it?"

"This place is like a basket of crabs. You'll get bitten before you know it."

"I wish you'd stop fussing. Am I supposed not to talk to anybody at all? Did you invite me over just to applaud you all the time?"

"I know what the situation is like around here."

"I'm sure you do – between doctors and patients. The man who knows it all."

They stood facing each other, chins raised. Their voices echoed in the bare hallway. The dogs yelped. Winston put his head round the corner, eyes popping with curiosity. A snap of the fingers was enough for him to dodge away.

Donald stomped back to the kitchen. "Damn. The dogs haven't been fed yet."

Mulder picked at his cactus spines. Painful, but Charmein's sting was worse. The only local for whom he felt anything resembling friendship, a whore? So Donald had another excuse to moralise: serious, fair-minded, know-it-all Donald, seething with unvoiced recriminations. But he had changed, dammit, he wasn't the old Marten who was forever breaking the rules. True, he had been careless with women. He wasn't the only one. God, how cocky they'd been in the old days, and how stupid. And thanks to that confounded village it was all coming back – all those bruised egos.

Donald retreated to his study. They would discuss things further during their walk the next day.

"Tomorrow morning at six?"

"Ja, baas."

They did not shake hands.

At the gate Mulder bumped into Winston, who was poking an awl into the lock. Somebody had been squirting resin again. It was a plague. He rummaged in a tin and picked out a new cylinder – from another house. He waved a bunch of keys, laughing. "I fixed Meneer's front door only yesterday."

Mulder's jaw dropped. Christ, come to think of it, his door key had turned very easily that morning.

Of course it had, and also the holes in Meneer's roof would soon be taken care of. Winston was the roof-man too.

Could he get in everywhere?

Of course he could. They all needed him up in the dunes.

The sun baked the puddles dry. Mulder looked up at the drifting clouds. The helicopter veered away from the coast towards the interior. A rainbow appeared. He walked back to his house at a brisk pace; he too had correspondence to see to, such as getting in touch with the pen-pal-seeking prisoner. Mulder had tucked the card from the supermarket noticeboard behind the bathroom mirror. It was a reminder. A souvenir. Each time he shaved he renewed his resolve to answer the ad. But what could one write to a man in a cell? Try to nourish him with descriptions of things he could no longer feel, hear, see or smell? The reek of smouldering seaweed, the blue of the dunes at sunset, the red skirt of an oyster-seller, her creaking basket ... or a prickly yellow cactus fruit, the scream of gulls, the wavy trail made by a snake in the sand ... No, too cruel. Better perhaps to stick to the beauties of corruption in politics, bribery scandals, secret arms deals. My oh my, fancy pimping for all that wickedness ...

There was no end to the deprivations of a prisoner: no festering sores of the city, no warm-blooded quarry, no fast bucks (still sticky with blood), no hanging onto a train with the wind in your hair. No space.

What a letter that would make! Should he really write all that stuff? His fingers were in no mood for typing, and his feet craved the freedom of the beach.

The sand was steaming and the bay made a desolate impression. Mulder walked along a ridge of seaweed and shells left behind by the tide. Crabs and gulls explored the freshly rinsed beach. The rain had erased all the tracks, save those of a lone walker. Somebody had been there before him. The footprints coming down from the dunes were still crisp at the edges. Quick feet, smallish, in flip-flops.

He followed the trail, covering the footprints with his own and trying to imagine what the other person was like, in terms of rhythm, voice, yearning. But the village was inescapable. He had come down to the beach for a breather, to clear his mind, and now the scene was becoming more oppressive by the minute: the dunes in the morning mist and the changing colour of the sand, the buoys heavy with seaweed, the fishermen drunk in the harbour, the boats lying idle on the slipway – and the plaintive women, and the daughters giving birth, and the poachers brandishing nail-sticks, and the whites behind their walls, and the tik-heads seeking solace in their hell.

Was this what they had dreamt of back in Paris? Why had Donald's hopes been reduced to this backwater?

He thought back on the comrades in France dancing a jig on the beach. They had been after something else entirely – freedom, not a community awash with the tide of stagnation. Equality, not a divided country where a new elite placed their own clan above others.

Mulder gazed at the seagulls, screaming and swooping over the waves. He heard the sound of singing . . .

He felt he was floating, borne aloft by voices. A party of elated Africans on the beach at Mont Saint-Michel. Women as well as men, comrades quite unknown to Donald and Marten, come from Paris by coach at the invitation of some rich widow, a champagne socialist and owner of a mansion on the coast. There had been food and drink, and a speech from the higher command in Algiers concerning the tasks awaiting them. Things would get better. Fairer. One man one vote. One constitution for all. South African citizenship for all, regardless of colour or clan. They were celebrating the Rainbow Nation on the beach. Mayibuye! May Africa return! An Africa without townships, without restricted areas of any kind. Share the problems, share the solutions. Africa resounded in every voice. Freedom was a song, a raised fist. Mayibuye! Donald sang at the top of his voice, he had been practising for weeks and his accent was the blackest of them all. Marten did not join in.

Mayibuye! They traced the word in the sand with their heels. Took pictures of it before the tide came in. For later. To take back home. Marten photographed them for the group portrait. No need for him to be in the picture: he wasn't from South Africa, had never even been there.

A man from Algiers took him aside, for the final instructions.

"What if I'm caught?"

"Sacrifice yourself," said the man from Algiers.

The trail of small-slippered footprints petered out among uprooted sea bamboo and plastic waste clotted with motor oil. Mulder had to screw up his eyes against the glare, which was intensifying as the clouds thinned. The sun glittered in the flying spray, blinding white, even the quicksand hurt his eyes. He had forgotten to bring his sunglasses, and his shoes were anything but waterproof.

No point in taking them off even if getting sand in his socks was a nuisance, because the beach was dotted with poisonous blue-bottle jellyfish, fragile-looking bubbles of transparent blue which left burns on your feet, even on the calluses. He considered turning back, but the dainty footprints held him captive. He would take his shoes off later, let them dry, massage his calf, lie down flat on his back in the sand, shut his eyes and stare at the sun from behind the shutters of skin, the way he used to do as a boy.

Land and sea flowed together. Mulder's vision became increasingly blurry, a side-effect of the blood-pressure pills, so he had to slow down. The slippers curved away from the tide-line and up to the soft dry sand, where walking was more arduous and the wind played havoc with the trail. He felt dizzy. His leg hit something and he stumbled. A basket rolled on its side, spilling shells onto the hot sand, empty perlemoen shells. There was also a white headscarf and a pair of flip-flops. But where had the feet gone?

Mulder took off his shoes and socks and splashed his face with seawater. His eyesight improved. Crests on the waves, rising spray. Was that a swimmer he could see? That dark blob framed by the surf? Who on earth would be reckless enough to take a swim here, among the sharp rocks, with a strong wind driving the foam back out to sea?

Had the head gone under, or was it already in the next cove?

Mulder shouted – but he sounded absurdly timid, as though embarrassed about standing there watching. What could he do anyway? Maybe this wasn't somebody just being reckless, maybe it was suicide. Imagine it was him, and he'd come all the way here to end it all in this godforsaken place and somebody got it into their head to rescue him! He'd drag the nosy parker down with him! A person was entitled to commit suicide undisturbed.

He walked back to the basket, picked up the scarf and waved it for a long time. Like a peace flag.

The sea was empty, shimmering white.

He sniffed at the scarf. Salty – from the shells. And sweet – the scarf of a woman. He draped it over his shoulders and sunburnt neck. Finder's keepers. A small erection presented itself. He dropped the slippers back in the basket. A quiet thud, and yet louder than the waves.

———

The village dozed in the late afternoon sun. Mulder was thirsty and decided to call at the hotel for a glass of beer. Besides, the cactus spines in his hand were itching again. The aloe was wearing off. He might be able to borrow a pair of tweezers from the doorman. The lobby was deserted. So was the bar. He wandered into the leafy courtyard and waited.

Three policemen appeared, deep in conversation. They glanced about and went back inside. Mulder trailed after them, in search of somebody who could supply him with a drink. There were more police in the dining room, all of them black except one, an older fellow standing aloof and apart, and the only one with rank insignia on his uniform. He and Mulder exchanged a nod and a faint smile, the way whites look at other whites when they are in the minority (or coloureds at other coloureds for that matter). Mulder lowered his eyes in embarrassment.

The lobby, the staircase – deserted. No guests, no staff in sight. Until he caught sight of a stooping figure in white overalls emerging from the lift. It was old Winston.

"Do you work here as well?"

Winston looked away. "I'm lending my grandson a hand."

"Does he work here?"

"Yes, in the bar. His name is Karneels."

Ah, the friendly bartender, so discreet.

But the bar was closed. The police were searching the hotel. Winston inspected Mulder's inflamed hand. Meneer needed to put some more aloe on it.

"Is it all because of the robbery?"

"The man who was robbed was a quota inspector. His brief-case with all his papers in it – it's gone," Winston said, going on to explain that the quota man had confiscated the cold store accounts because the energy bill was too high. It didn't tally with the bans on fishing boats leaving the harbour. The fuel depot had been sealed.

Any trace of the culprit yet?

Winston shrugged. "Rumours, rumours." The staff were being questioned in the conference room. Karneels too, only because he'd taken a bottle of vodka up to the man's room – at the mayor's instruction. Oh sure, blame the under-village again . . . The police were taking it very seriously, the quota inspector had friends in high places.

Winston checked whether the coast was clear and let Mulder into the bar. The refrigerators were locked. Sorry, no beer. But he happened to have a key to the liquor cupboard. "Shall I pour Meneer a tot, then?"

He was drunk. From two glasses of J.&B., from his walk, from the cactus spines and all the other worries. Winston poured a mean drink, the devil. And brimmed with gossip. Mulder was briefed about his neighbours up the road in detail. Stienie was in possession of a vibrator. Not a word about the Doctor though.

Mulder stood at the foot of his dune dreading the climb. He felt a pang of guilt thinking of the head bobbing in the waves and the white headscarf left on the beach. Should he go and check whether Charmein was at home, safe and sound?

He walked back to no-man's-land, scarf in hand to fend off stray dogs. The harbour was deserted. Two young policemen, youths from Distriksdorp, stood on guard by the cold store. The shops were closed. The bakery woman was sweeping her stoep. Did she happen to know where Charmein lived? The woman fled into the house and locked the door. He asked a fisherman, who pretended not to hear. In the end he accosted a teenager carrying a long nail-stick. He had worked out how to deal with the local kids by now. Ten rand and he'd be shown the way.

Charmein lived at the bottom of the under-village, where the peeling walls were splattered with mud and the street lamps were broken. It was not far. His guide knew the way like the back of his hand, kept the dogs at bay and shielded him from importunate stick-wielding mates. They stopped in front a house with a shiny corrugated roof. It was less dingy than its neighbours and even had net curtains at the windows, as white as the scarf. The boy didn't dare venture into the yard, but that was where Charmein, the "Cape Townie" lived. Would Meneer manage to find his way home again in the dark?

"I won't be long." Mulder said.

The door stood ajar. Mulder knocked, waited in suspense. He turned the handle; it squeaked. It was dark inside. Again he smelled the strange smell, a mixture of clammy sea air and sweet oil. "Charmein! Charmein!" he called, too loudly for the size of the house. He gave the scarf a squeeze and saw himself standing on the beach again, crying and whispering to the waves. He pushed the door open. It was a while before he could see anything. A bed with a shiny yellow frame. Was it occupied? Mulder shrank back, shut the door and walked around the house. At the back he heard soft music coming from a shed in the yard. The door was open. Inside, the floor was strewn with old magazines, the walls were covered in photographs. In a deckchair lounged a boy, fast asleep. Pink sneakers, right arm in plaster.

Mulder knocked on the door. Hendrik sat up with a jolt.

"Is your mother at home?"

"I . . . dunno."

"Is there anyone with her in the house?"

"Dunno." Hendrik didn't know a thing. He had a vague, numbed look.

"Do you remember me?"

"Sort of." The ride to town, the hospital . . . ah yes, it was dawning on him. He could do with a lift again, he said. The village was closed, and he needed to go to town. Or else, could Meneer lend him a bit of cash?

"I'm looking for Charmein. Is she taking a rest?"

Hendrik shambled to the front of the house and kicked the door wide open.

The bed did not move. On the pillows sat a family of toy bears. Pandas, big ones, small ones, pandas with little hats on and T-shirts saying, "I ♥ Taiwan". Hendrik took a box of matches from his pocket and lit a lamp. Still more animals loomed up, a side-table full of them: a porcelain cat lifting a golden front paw, a hedgehog wearing lederhosen, a monkey made of coconut-shell, and also a miniature Big Ben and ditto pagoda – souvenirs from harbours the world over, all bathed in a soft paraffin glow.

Mulder held up the white scarf. "Does this belong to your mother?"

Hendrik hunched his shoulders. "Does Meneer fancy my ma?"

"No. Could she have lost it?"

Too bad for Meneer. Hendrik cupped his hand for a tip.

Mulder shook his head, dropped the scarf on Charmein's bed and walked out of the door. Hendrik asked him to wait a moment; he went to the shed and returned with a black briefcase – artificial leather, gilt corner reinforcements. Not expensive-looking.

"Where did that come from?"

"Found it in the dunes."

Mulder clicked the lid open. Empty, except for a side pocket containing a ballpoint. Blue logo: *Fishing Unlimited*.

"Shall I bring it to the police for you?"

"O.K. Meneer." Hendrik handed over the briefcase. He had imitated Mulder's accent surprisingly well. They both had to smile. Then he put on a different voice, whining, with eyes narrowed to slits and beads of sweat on his upper lip. "I'm so sick, Meneer! Ach Meneer, gimme ten rand."

"I can give you food, medicines . . . Perhaps you should see a doctor."

No, no, Hendrik didn't need a doctor, just a little cash. His ma wouldn't give him anything. Fok. And Meneer? Meneer was loaded, like everybody from overseas. Fok, fok, fok. He seized the briefcase and ran off, weaving between the houses.

The under-village awoke from its afternoon nap. Mulder was exhausted and sweaty from roaming the dank settlement, where it smelled of brackish water. He longed for the cool breeze up on the dunes and for his sofa by the open window.

Children and dogs swarmed to the harbour, too hasty to bother him. Mothers lit small fires, girls went about gathering kindling – always the women and their diligent daughters. One girl, blacker than her peers, carried a large barracuda on her head – a leaking hat.

A sea wind arose. Mulder went past the prayer hall, where pious matrons in white headscarves were gathered for vespers. Charmein was not among them. Poachers and smugglers rode their buggies round the harbour, tik-heads crawled out of their warrens and youngsters darted about the boats on the slipway, keeping track of demand and supply. Mulder watched from a distance. Where were the fishermen, the fathers?

On the wasteland next to the hotel he noticed a boy sitting under a tree with his legs wide apart and his head lolling on his chest. He seemed to have difficulty breathing. Mulder went up to him, but there was no reaction from the boy. His trousers were caked with filth, and a dribble of vomit ran down his chin. Under the same tree, round an upturned oil drum with a bottle placed at the centre, sat four men playing cards. When he drew their attention to the boy they laughed, showing gold teeth as well as toothless gums. He couldn't stand the sight of them. Useless fathers.

Mulder called his bank in Paris, or rather, Madame Toussaint of the rue de Médicis branch, who, being aware that Monsieur never read his bank statements, kindly kept an eye on his modest holdings for him.

"How much money have I got left?"

"How long do you expect to live?"

"That bad, is it?"

"Falling markets."

The line crackled.

"Nothing ventured, nothing gained."

Madame Toussaint giggled – it was their private joke. She asked about the weather at the Cape, and in return told him that the Jardin de Luxembourg was strewn with chestnuts and the asters were still in flower, but that the palm trees had already been moved into the orangerie . . .

In his mind's eye Mulder saw the chalky glass of the green-houses, he saw the orchids, the dovecote, the shorn hedges, and the statues which, when the weather turned cold, were given straw jackets to wear. How many gardeners worked there? Four or five dozen, he thought. Full time. As a matter of course. Alleys swept, litter collected – daily. Reliable mail delivery. A metro every four minutes. Went without saying.

"How about me paying for Hendrik's education?" Mulder said.

Donald's stick dropped from his hand. He was standing on the highest point of the headland, about to trace the outline of the "eye of the sea", the expanse of ocean between the Cape and the South Pole, where you could see a storm gathering days before it reached the shore.

"Hendrik is being taken care of."

"He'll have to go to a detox clinic first, which is bound to be pretty expensive, and besides he may need more help in future. If I pay for his studies, his grant can go to someone else."

Donald scowled. "What's with all this concern about some boy you haven't met more than a couple of times at the outside? Is it because of Charmein?"

"I care about this country too, you know."

"You don't know what you're talking about."

"You taught me a lot about South Africa in the old days."

"You mean during your flirtation with the Struggle?" Donald tossed the stick away, the dogs lunged after it. "Don't make me laugh. Your struggle was a diversion."

"Look who's talking! Acting the revolutionary abroad and leaving the fighting to people who couldn't afford a plane ticket."

The entire morning walk had gone by without any allusion to the previous day's disagreement, and now they were glaring at each other again, chins thrust forward.

"I mean to help that boy," Mulder said. "And that's final."

Donald stared grimly at the sea. "Just leave his mother alone, will you?"

"No, I'll go and bed her under your nose."

Donald took a deep breath. "I'm only trying to be supportive, show you the ropes in this complicated community. A practice run for our trip, shall we say, but you keep getting all emotional. There's a difference between having a guilty conscience and a sense of responsibility. Think about it."

"Noble white guy," Mulder said.

"Thrill-seeker." Donald whistled the dogs and stalked off. "Let me know when you need a lift to the airport."

Mulder went in the opposite direction. The dogs were puzzled, ran from the one to the other, shivery tails between their legs. They could sense the anger. Mulder chased them away: he no longer needed an escort.

Bacon and eggs. Mulder decided to have breakfast at the hotel, nice and greasy and filling, no awkward conversations. Even more appealing was the idea of flushing down the aftertaste of discord with a drink at the bar. There were bound to be a couple of delivery men from Distriksdorp there; he would join their idle gossip about cricket and the latest starlet in the *Daily Sun*. Anything to avoid being stuck on a sand-dune with nothing to do.

Not a cloud in the sky, not a wrinkle in the sea. The village still seemed to be sleeping. The pier glistened in the morning light, still wet from the receding tide. He headed off towards the harbour. Common sense had prevailed: a swim first, then food. In this weather he had no need of a towel, and his boxer shorts could easily withstand the calm sea. Making his way among the boats, he noticed that he was not alone. There was a boy asleep in a dinghy, mouth agape, one arm hanging limply over the side. Was he dead? Mulder bent over him. Stench of vomit, urine-stained trousers, ragged shirt. But he was breathing.

Mulder had qualms about getting undressed near the sleeping

boy. He made for the pier, and was hailed on the way by an old woman. She was looking for Riempie, her grandson.

"There's somebody in one of those boats. He's asleep." He walked back with her to show her where.

Sure enough, it was Riempie.

She shook him awake. Riempie opened his eyes a fraction. Mulder asked the woman if she needed help.

No, she was used to it, all the searching, all the waiting. "Riempie hides from my eyes." She wiped the dirt off his face. "Just look at him, all yellow, so feeble."

Mulder felt uneasy and wanted to leave.

"He was such a lively little boy," she said. "Like a sand-hopper." The wind had got hold of him and now there was no tying him down. "He's out of control, Meneer."

She had hoped things would have turned out the other way round: for him to wash her when she got old. "I'm so tired," she said. "Too tired to go on mothering him."

The Living Shores of Southern Africa lay in the heat behind the windowpane, curling at the edges. Mulder had spent the entire afternoon on the sofa reading the book, and was utterly sick of it. Things were even worse under water than they were on dry land. No wonder the fishermen drank. He drew the curtains and uncorked a bottle of Allesverloren wine – an hour before sundowner time.

As he was locking the front door – securing the extra bolt – he noticed an envelope lying in the hallway. Slipped under the door, apparently. It contained a sheet of paper covered in numbers separated by dots and commas: 3.111,23,15,214,33;3X. He recognised it as the Cuban code, but was too tipsy to read anything into it. The numbers referred to lines and letters in a book, that much he knew. Which book could it be? In Paris they had used the English Bible, the King James version, and it wasn't as if they were stone-cold sober then either. Doing the deciphering was a bit tedious, but you could pick any book you liked – all you had to do was agree on which one. On the back of the note there was another code: A.B.PS.60:3,2,4. The clue to the book, obviously. Which book would they both have at hand? *Living Shores*? He didn't think he had mentioned it to Donald.

A Bible then? He had come across one when he was cleaning the house, had even considered hiding his credit card in it, but then decided not to, as it would be tempting fate. After hunting around for a quarter of an hour he found it lying on the bottom shelf of his bedside cabinet: Die Afrikaanse Bijbel. That was what the A.B. stood for. He located Psalm 60 in no time: a prayer of hope after defeat.

He took a pencil and held it poised over the text until the wine began to wear off. Verse three: line one, 11th letter = S. Line two, 3rd letter = K. Line one, 5th letter = U. Line two, 14th letter = another U. Line three, 3rd letter = S. The word was SKUUS. Afrikaans for sorry, multiplied by three.

After half an hour he had succeeded in spelling out the actual message. *We leave tomorrow. This place is driving us both crazy. Everything will be fine. P.S. if you can unravel this your memory must be O.K.*

D onald spread the map on the bonnet of the car. "Look, there's the river. We're just here on this mountain, that's Stellenbosch on the right. You were living right by this railway station." The paper flapped wildly in the wind, but the sturdy canvas backing kept it from tearing. Mulder pored over the markings on a vintage topographic map of a section of the Western Cape. Special Branch standard, rubber-stamped on the back by the secret service. Classified information. Anything of the remotest strategic importance was minutely indicated: military barracks, police stations, railway lines, schools, fire stations, hospitals, as well as every location requiring extra surveillance in times of emergency or unrest, such as radio transmitters, prisons, coloured and black areas. The wavy lines on the map made Mulder's head spin, and he had to steady himself against Donald's car. He needed a holdfast for his memory.

"So where was the arms cache?"

Donald's finger traced the winding lines of old roads long since widened and straightened. "Real secrets weren't marked on it, of course. That's where your powers of recall come in."

Mulder looked around him, dazed from trying to find his bearings on the map, or just dazed in general, as he frequently felt anyway. Neither the map nor his memory corresponded with the landscape. Where they were standing ought to be grass and sand, indicated with yellow and green hatching on the map. But the population of the Cape had overturned the strictures of the old regime, and now the vast plains were being built up. The borders between cities and townships had become blurred; the colour codes no longer corresponded with reality. He bent over the map once more. Ah, so this must have been where he hiked through the wilderness with his soldier-mates from the boarding house. It had been a clear day, and they had been able to see the Hottentots-Holland mountains in the distance. Boozed up with beer, they had written their names with bullet holes in sheets of corrugated iron. And they had made a braai under a eucalyptus tree.

Old landscapes came into focus again. Donald had predicted as much: "It's your fear of forgetting that's blocking your memory. Everything you experienced back then is locked away somewhere in your brain, we just need to find the key to the lock."

Mulder took a deep breath. He felt goosebumps spreading over his arms.

Donald tapped him on the shoulder. "Let's get moving, it'll be dark before we know it." He began folding the map, carefully.

"And you hung on to it for all these years!"

"It's the only thing I inherited from my pa. Of course, I made sure I got my hands on it well before he died."

Mulder sniffed the canvas backing. "So I had this whole map in my head, right?"

Donald grinned. "Ten inches of it max. I know I drummed it into you."

Mulder searched for a wine stain or some other trace of the nights they had spent practising map-reading in Paris, in preparation for his journey. He was supposed to know his way around with military exactitude. From memory, because he couldn't take the map with him. He sat day after day with a ruler, checking the millimetres separating the barracks. This was "The Knowledge", as Donald called it, borrowing the term from the requirements for a London cab driver's licence. It was all about training that part of the brain where spatial memory is stored. The *posterior hippocampus*. A typically Donald-ish term.

But whose spatial memory could take into account the advent of bulldozers and the spread of black suburbs?

They were driving towards Stellenbosch, where Mulder had wasted so much time as a student. He would find his way around there much more easily, given that he had spent so much time tearing around the old town on the motorbike belonging to his landlady's son. All things being equal, there should be a military barracks not far from a wine cooperative, halfway between two townships – one for blacks, one for coloureds. Just a small army unit, whose main task was to keep the rabble in order. Mulder had been there once, in the mess, with his boarding-house mates. He had drawn a very passable map of the terrain – one of his first assignments.

The road took them through built-up areas not indicated on their map. They got lost. They asked directions, received confusing replies, and eventually discovered that the barracks had been demolished years ago. Donald said they would take Du Toit Street, go past the boarding house where Mulder used to live. It was now a smart villa.

"I'd never have found it by myself," Mulder remarked, sunk in thought. After a pause he said, "How did you know the name of the street? I never told anybody."

"We kept a close eye on you."

Mulder did not dare pursue the subject.

Conversation was still at a cautious stage. They had made up their quarrel (a handshake, a crooked grin, and that was that), but the atmosphere was still somewhat strained. Donald had dismissed the incident; he'd had a lot on his mind, too much hassle. Time to take a day off.

Although Mulder had been looking forward to a change of scene, packing his rucksack had proved stressful, and not only due to his quantities of pills. Was there really any point in resuscitating the old Marten? The name that was supposed to restore his youth and strength was only making him feel older, what with all the extra ballast weighing him down. Overcome with dread at the moment of departure, he had played for time by pointing out that Donald's 4x4 stank of wet dog, and had set about wiping the upholstery with an array of cleaning products. It did not make him feel any better. Nor did the dogs, who eyed him balefully throughout. He was glad they would be staying behind. Winston would look after them.

No sooner had they left the village behind than Mulder confessed to having doubts. Wouldn't it be better to turn back?

"What? Don't tell me you want to back out now!"

"Hendrik might need you."

"His mother and I have got things sorted."

"But she wasn't at home."

"How did you know that? Horny dog."

Mulder told him about the small footprints on the beach, the head lost in the surf, the white scarf, the briefcase.

Donald told him not to worry: Charmein was fine. She had phoned him that very morning.

"About Hendrik?"

Yes, the poor woman had been worried sick, all those police descending on the village, all because of one missing briefcase.

That was why she had come to the gate in a panic. "I gave her some pills for Hendrik to calm him down and made arrangements with a detox clinic. Privately run. They came early this morning to pick him up. So he's under the radar as far as the police are concerned. Not much else we can do for the time being, is there?"

———

"Last day, first choice," said a sign along the road. Donald and Mulder had already driven past it twice, and now they saw it again, at the bottom of a driveway marked with whitewashed stones. An arrow pointed to a small house on a hill. People lingered among randomly parked cars. Two men were carrying a sofa out of the house. Bleating goats were tethered to a post.

Donald stopped to ask directions, as Mulder's map-reading skills had become rusty. He had confused a tarred road with a railway line: just two tiny strokes' difference, but enough to take them more than an hour out of their way. The sun was already setting behind the hills.

It turned out to be the last day for Oom Koosie and Tannie Rosa, an elderly couple who were leaving their farm for good. The soil was starved and the harvest very poor. After years of drudgery they had been forced to sell their farm, on the orders of the bank and below its real value. Now they were selling off their possessions. And where would they be going?

Bellville: you could still find a cheap place to rent in the crowded Cape suburbs, explained Tannie Rosa. But yes, she would miss the wide open spaces.

Badly?

Yes, but not *that* badly. Even if they could do with some more Rands.

Second-hand dealers drifted through the house, complete

strangers who combed the countryside in their pickups. A field day for bargain hunters. A young couple rummaged in the kitchen drawers, but only wanted the barbecue set. They offered twenty rand for a rocking chair. "Belonged to my Grandpa," Tannie Rosa said. Maybe Oom Koosie would still want to sit in it.

Ah well, sitting around too much made you stiff, and that was worse.

Everything had to go. The fridge, a well-thumbed *Cook and Enjoy*, a straw hat – "belonged to my ma" – baby clothes she had completely forgotten about. Even the chickens were being sold, preferably to someone who wanted them for the eggs and not to wring their necks straight off. Tannie smiled as she shambled about. She stroked a pair of rickety chairs. Ten rand each. One dealer wanted a discount. "What, what?" She didn't have her hearing aid in.

"Being deaf has its compensations."

And having strangers sitting on her chairs and loading her brass bed into their pickup?

It was not the end of the world.

Of course, she would rather have passed her things on to the children, but they had emigrated. It was the will of God. And the neighbours six miles down the road were moving too. After having being robbed twice.

You had to accept it.

Yes, the area was changing fast. "It's gone very black around here." Was it alright for her to say that? Anyway, people always went looking for happiness in different places, which wasn't such a bad thing. But the loneliness, your own folks moving away, the empty pews on Sunday, the dead telephone, nobody listening to your complaints, no longer being able to find your language on the radio, having become a foreigner in your own country . . .

Yes, that was bad.

A chilly wind blew over the plain, vultures circled over the road. Mulder and Donald stared ahead glumly: they had been sent in the wrong direction. The topographical map was no help, as they were outside the charted area. The car radio crackled because of a loose contact. From behind the wheel Donald was trying to send a text message, but there was no signal. An hour later they were in the hills. They saw the first signs of civilisation: a rusty billboard, a neon-lit roadside restaurant. They decided to stop for a drink and discuss what to do.

It was too cold to sit out on the patio. Inside, the waiters were clearing the tables. Could they still order a drink?

Well, a quick one then, at the bar, because it was closing time. Donald picked up an old newspaper and, without thinking, asked for a bottle of wine. The best. Yes, a bottle. In that case they were invited to sit down by the window, but no lights would be turned on or the boss would have problems with his licence.

The evening crept over the table. Donald leafed though *Die Burger*. Ah, news about the village! At last! Together they pored over the page of regional news. CRIME AND FOUL PLAY. *Fishermen blame law-breaking on quotas, claim they have no other way of feeding and clothing their families.* The picture of the boat wreck sat alongside. Not a word about the quota inspector, though.

Donald's mobile rang. Ah, a signal! A voice message from Winston. The screen lit up in the dusk. He listened, shaking his head. "They've spread tar all over the gate."

"Should we go back?"

"What difference would that make? Winston will clean it tomorrow."

The wine was poured in the half-light. They could barely distinguish each other's faces.

"I admire you," Mulder said.

"How so?"

"For sticking it out there."

Donald said nothing; he was fumbling in his pockets.

"Anything wrong?" Mulder said.

"Sorry. No, I was thinking of Sarah: she never took to the place either. She wants to move back to France, she's making me choose between her and South Africa."

Mulder tried to show sympathy, but mumbled the words, while the pat on the shoulder he intended to give became an empty wave in the gloom.

"I'm not leaving. Not again." Donald blew his nose. "No more homesickness for me. When I was a boy I never doubted that I'd live in South Africa all my life – in Pretoria, in the same street, safely among my own people. Nobody doubted that. We were content in our own little world. Servants were part of our lives – yes baas, no baas. I was small-baas. Not a clue whether they had children of their own – one didn't ask them personal questions. I didn't even know how to say hello in their language."

They each took a gulp of wine. Flashing lights came past: police cars.

"It was not until I went to university that I shed my cocoon," Donald went on. "University of Cape Town, English-speaking – an unusual choice in my family, but that was where the best medical training was to be had. At the clinic I got to know black patients, people who had been torn away from their families, driven apart by our laws. It was a revelation: all those men and women on the jam-packed trains to and from the townships had ceased to be a nameless, faceless crowd. I began to read about their longing for freedom. I wanted to be free myself."

A waiter stacked chairs on top of tables, another began swabbing the floor with peevish deliberation. Donald swore under his breath and continued reminiscing.

"We were worried about Africa. There was trouble at the borders, Angola, Mozambique, Rhodesia. Freedom fighters, but to us they were terrorists, baby-burners and rapists. We belonged to Europe, and we barricaded ourselves behind our Germanic language, our Calvinist heritage, our Roman law. We asked ourselves fearful questions, but never aloud: When will the hordes turn against us? How long will we go on being the boss? I was scared, too. Scared I'd turn out to be exactly like my pa: a defender of *Die Volk*'s values ... The army wanted me."

"And you were a crack shot," Mulder murmured.

"Don't rub it in. Yes, I fled to Paris, to break free. My country came second – that is, until I was consumed by homesickness."

Donald poured the last of the wine. Mulder had never heard his friend talk in this way. "You didn't mention any of these things at Fraternité."

"Because we weren't supposed to have a past of our own. It was all about the future. Besides, I had sworn not to pine for South Africa. My love had turned to hate, but when I was working with those black guys and we listened to their music, people like Dollar Brand, Hugh Masekela, Miriam Makeba, I felt more at ease with them than I ever did with all those crazy Frenchies. It was in Europe that I discovered that Africa was where I belonged."

Mulder clapped his hand to the side of his head. "Remember that time I took you to the club in Barbès? Packed with Senegalese every Friday night. You had never danced with a black girl before,

118

and you couldn't get enough of it! I can just see you now, drawing the outline of your country on a paper napkin. *Moi aussi, je suis un Africain*, you said, which the girls thought hilarious."

"Yeah," Donald said morosely, "but in Africa I turn all European again."

"And South Africa's becoming more and more African."

Donald thumped his fist on the table. "But things weren't better back then! They were not!"

The glasses shook. A young waitress appeared, startled. He ordered another bottle of wine. His tone was commanding.

"But I'm dammed if I'm going to complain. Not like all those people you've been talking to, your scared neighbours, those mates of yours at the hotel bar, yes, even Charmein. Sure, there was less crime on the streets back then, which is no wonder with half the population being banished at night. Have all those moaners of today forgotten the crimes committed in the past?"

Mulder wanted to ask a question, but Donald took no notice.

"I mean the crimes committed in the name of law and order. Raids, letter bombs, the poisoning of political opponents, detainees falling to their death from the top floor of the police station, the endless rows of children's graves in the arid homelands . . ."

"What about Tannie Rosa?"

"Tannie Rosa joined the queue just like me that day in April, under the bluest sky you can imagine, along with all the other people who came to vote for the first time in their lives. Farmers waited in line beside their workers, pink, powdered old ladies beside black gays with nose rings, garbage collectors beside nannies. People who had never dared to speak to each other became fellow citizens overnight."

Mulder leaned forward. "I asked you about Tannie Rosa."

119

"You should have seen us! There we were, congratulating each other. Because things were better before?" Donald gave a hollow laugh.

The waitress came with the bill.

"Is Tannie Rosa a complainer?"

"Ah well, the tannies . . . everybody falls for a dear old tannie." Donald pushed his chair back. "It's all going a bit too fast for the old folks, perhaps, but which of us doesn't feel like a stranger in his own country from time to time? It's just," he took a deep breath, "it's just that sometimes I'm scared I'll end up leaving too."

"*Having* to leave."

"Stop it, stop it, please." He drank the last drop of his glass and went over to the bar to pay, lurching a little. He snapped at the waitress.

A few kilometres down the road they came across Vineyard Cottage, with a notice outside offering lodging plus meals. A bite to eat would do them good. Without bothering to freshen up first, they settled themselves at a table as far removed as possible from the wedding party in the garden room, where a loud speech was underway. It was in Afrikaans, and ended with a call to prayer. Young and old held hands. Mulder watched from afar with amusement. He could just hear God joining the wedding feast, a peasant god who would bless the harvest – not too much rain, not too dry. "And, Lord, give reason and wisdom to those who rule our country."

Donald leafed through the menu, frowning. "That's what it was like in my family too."

Outside, dogs barked at the sky, pocket torches lit up. They discussed what they would eat; conversation flagged. Mulder let his eyes wander over the restaurant, he tried to catch what the people at the next table were saying. He noted that all the diners were white, and all the staff black, and said so.

"Spoils the appetite a bit."

"Is that what you say in Paris too? With all those illegals in the kitchens . . ."

The waitress placed a basket of bread between them. Mulder ordered spring water, Donald insisted on wine. From the garden room came a resounding chorus of amens: the prayer had ended.

Donald took a long draught from his glass. "I can still feel my pa's dry hand gripping mine at mealtimes when he led us in prayer for minutes on end."

"When did you last see him?"

"Once he found out what I was doing in Paris I was persona non grata. My mother wrote to me a few times, hoping to convert me. In the end I broke with the entire family. My eldest sister lives in New Zealand, I believe. My mother died when she was sixty; my pa died before the changeover. I saw a notice in the paper. In those days I couldn't enter the country anymore." He gave Mulder a searching look. "You knew my pa worked for the Ministry of Justice, didn't you, mister spy?"

Rattled, Mulder stared outside, but all he could see was his reflection in the black windowpane. Short grey hair, bespoke shirt – a distinguished-looking gentleman trying hard to put himself in the shoes of the rebel he once was. "Yes I did, but it didn't go any further. I never mentioned it to anyone."

The waitress turned up for the second time to take their orders. Mulder chose a simple dish. Donald ordered a second bottle of wine. He had no appetite for food.

Family was a taboo topic at Fraternité: the less you knew about each other, the safer it was. You didn't invite people to your lodgings, you didn't ask where people came from or where they lived. Not easy for exiles from the same country, but everybody on the course abided by that rule. And Donald was strict. But by the end of the first week Marten, a loner and political ignoramus, knew a great deal more than he was supposed to know.

It had been a complete cock-up. The Chief had procured him a temporary address, a book-filled attic on the edge of Les Halles, the wholesale market area that was being demolished at the time. The bowels of Paris laid bare beneath his window. The occupant had left the place in a shambles of papers, magazines, political tracts. While he was clearing up, Mulder came across a shoebox filled with newspaper cuttings under the bed. The language was Afrikaans: parliamentary reports, articles on censorship, law and order, with red underlinings. There was also a grainy newspaper photograph of a man in uniform addressing a crowd of men wearing hats. The caption said it was Karel Treghardt. Even more intriguing were the papers at the bottom of the box: two bundles of letters addressed to Faan Treghardt. Marten read them diagonally, in keeping with his status of trainee spy. Curious to find more, he rummaged in drawers and cupboards and found a South African passport in the name of Stephanus Louis Treghardt. Marten recognised the square jaw and piercing eyes in the photograph, in spite of the close-cropped hair. Donald, the mentor assigned to him by Fraternité. How could this be?

Weeks later, Marten confronted Donald with his real name. They were doing experiments with *encre sympathique*, writing notes to each other in onion juice and starchy water. Exposing the paper to heat or wiping it with a cotton swab dipped in iodine made the message appear in brown: *Faan ek ken jou naam*. I know your name.

"You went as white as a sheet," Mulder said. He recalled the scene in vivid detail, which even now afforded him a degree of schadenfreude. "You hurled the iodine bottle at me. I couldn't get the stain off my neck for days."

"The place was meant for some Algerian originally, not for you at all."

Mulder raised his glass: "To the fastidious activist." Still, that was when they had become friends, wasn't it? "It was because I knew where you came from that you dared to speak to me in Afrikaans."

"You'd hit on my weak spot, and you could easily have exploited it."

"Oh, of course, betrayal was on the tip of my tongue. The South African embassy would have paid a tidy sum for information about the son of a leading apartheid ideologist being instructed in revolutionary practice at a communist training camp," Mulder said, grinning. "Which was not inconvenient."

"How do you mean?"

"Power. You were better than me at everything. You were more intelligent, you had more self-control, and yet your fate was in my hands."

"So I was clasping an adder to my breast." Donald made to stand up.

"Don't get me wrong. If you're weak, you turn to someone who's stronger for support. By not betraying you I could be a better person. You gave me the opportunity to be on the right side. Thanks to you I could be part of a war of liberation."

"You had already made that choice. Why else did you join Fraternité?"

"I was drawn into it."

"By Catherine?"

"Let's not talk about her."

"Why not? You behave as if she never existed."

Catherine was Marten's – Mulder's and nobody else's, for all that he'd had to share her with dozens of people. She had touched him, lifted him up – words that would have undoubtedly made her laugh. She was talking about her country the first time he saw her, at that bookshop in Paris. He caught the word "apartheid", which sounded so Dutch that he stopped to listen. He was struck by her intensity. And by her appearance, which had nothing of the keyed-up activist about it, rather of the society girl championing the cause of exploited blacks. Annoying, he thought, but she had a pleasant voice – compelling yet soft – and she was beautiful and elegant with her upswept blond hair and her white fluttery skirt. He only understood half of what she was saying, as his French was still shaky, but he was impressed anyway: by her love of South Africa, of the people, the landscape, and the way she spoke of injustice with a smile on her face. He might well have moved on and not taken her at her word had he not been in Africa himself a few months earlier . . .

He had sailed up the Nile in a slow-moving dhow toward Wadi Halfa, a trip costing just a few piastres, affordable for a twenty-year-old with plenty of time and a yen for adventure. It had rained for weeks, he had been eaten alive by mosquitoes, and he had seen real-life Nubians, negroes like the ones pictured in the *National Geographic*, men of gleaming ebony who invited him into their huts. He inhaled the aromas of cooking fires and red, dewy mud, and believed he had fallen in love with Africa. Khartoum was only two or three days away by road. He could hitchhike. He might even go further south, why not? A lorry driver gave him a lift to the city, and upon arrival he wandered off into the chaos, full of expectation. It was the first time in his life that he saw true poverty. Unlike in Egypt, here the slums had no electricity or running water, even the old colonial centre was filthy and decrepit. Children ate mud, men chewed leaves. The muezzin shrilled louder here, and more slippers were strewn on the steps of the mosque. A man spat on the ground before his feet, boys made obscene gestures, bus drivers honked when they saw him. A strange place. He saw a banner on the gate of a large hotel: BRITISH GO HOME. There was a small gathering of whites by the entrance: backpackers like him, business-men, humanitarian aid workers, diplomats. What was going on? A riot. An English soccer coach had offended Sudan, not just by letting the national team lose, but also with a comment made during an interview, about "the boys behaving like monkeys". The coach, whose wife was African, was put on the first flight out. The embassy had lodged an official complaint, after which every white was a racist. There was more behind it: a conflict with British Petroleum, but for the outside world it was Sudan's honour that was at stake.

He laughed it all off and went on his way. The cheap hotels had no vacancies, at least not for him. The eateries turned him away. Today not for British. Suddenly he was a Brit, too. The spitting increased. Somebody poked him from behind. Before dark he was back at the expensive hotel where he had spoken to the whites. He was lucky to be offered a bed for the night by an aid worker. The next day he flew back to Luxor.

Home again, he felt the Sudanese had a point: an eye for an eye, a tooth for a tooth. The trials faced by him in a single day – well fed and clothed and having enough money to make his escape – were what Africans had been living with for centuries. The colour of a person's skin carried more implications than he had reckoned with.

He began to read – travel books mainly – and discovered the sources of the Nile. Without porters, regrettably, for there was a colonial inside him wanting to get out. He also read about how the European powers had divided up the continent like slicing a cake, straight across languages and kingdoms. He wanted to understand the consequences: not the knife, but the wound.

During a holiday in Paris he stumbled upon a bookshop called *Présence Africaine* in the rue des Écoles. A meeting place of writers and students, young intellectuals from West Africa and the Congo seeking companionship. A bespectacled Africa – no sign of gleaming Nubians or tom-tom drumming peoples in touch with Nature.

And there she stood, fluttery white skirt, blond hair, long legs. It was spring, and Paris was buzzing with activity. She spoke in praise of a book entitled *Pleure, o pays bien aimé*, the French translation of Alan Paton's *Cry, the Beloved Country*. The Africans in the bookshop hadn't heard of it, but they all feasted their eyes on her. The young man at the till called her by her first name. Catherine bought five copies, which she handed out. A well-intentioned gesture, but somehow irritating.

She bought more books, signed a cheque with a flourish (in lilac ink), and had the parcel taken to her car, a pale-blue cabriolet. All eyes were on her; the shop held its breath. A dog wandered off into the street. Traffic was heavy, and the dog was scooped up by a bus. It flew through the air, yelping in agony. Catherine ran to it and gathered it up in her wide skirt. Blood seeped through the white fabric, trickled down her long bare legs. She placed the wounded animal on the back seat of the car. Pale upholstery, now bloodstained. And off she went, in the direction of the boulevard Saint Michel. The Africans standing on the pavement watched open-mouthed as she pulled away: "*Quelle femme!*"

The stains on her skirt were etched on his memory. Catherine was the kind of woman who would hide you if you were on the run.

The staff of Vineyard Cottage hung around at the far end of the restaurant. The wedding party had left. In the garden room the tables were being laid for the following day with much rattling of cutlery. The two men pretended not to notice. They were indulging in gossip. Especially Mulder, who was anxious to avoid the subject of Catherine. "Remember that weird woman with a harelip who vanished from one day to the next? She had an Irish accent, I seem to remember, and every time we sat down to a meal she insisted the food was better in East Germany. I wonder why she was in such a hurry to leave."

"Sent packing by the organisation," Donald said. "She was working for British Intelligence."

And Paulus, the young black who wrote protest poems under five different aliases? "*The imperialist moon rose over the capitalist landscape*" flashed across Mulder's mind.

"Knee-capped." He sold Bibles in Port Elizabeth nowadays.

They delved into the past, while sparing themselves. They became increasingly animated, the way they used to be in the cafés, but in the Vineyard Cottage dining room their talk sounded brash and over-loud.

The drink seeped deeper into their memories. The medieval manuscript cropped up, the audacious theft from the old Bibliothèque Nationale.

"It was a crazy idea," Donald said. "I don't know where you got it from."

"We needed money."

"To save lives, yes, not to put other people at risk. The risk you took was outrageous. Your description was in all the papers." Donald looked stern; recalling Marten's ineptitude had a sobering effect on him.

"But I was good at being invisible," Mulder said. "That was my speciality: being there by not being there."

"You had to go: Duriez wanted to get rid of you. Just as well you already had your visa for South Africa, so you could leave within a week. Panic all round. That so-called mission of yours was actually more of an escape."

"Duriez, did you say?" Mulder pulled a face. "Duriez . . . I'd blocked him out altogether. What a fraud. But we used to call him the Chief, right? You rather liked him. How could you? He was a fanatic. He was always saying, 'La politique avant le peuple.' Besides, he pinched the girls' bottoms."

The two friends exchanged awkward looks. Yes, well, they'd had a couple of wild months together. Women, too much to drink, free access to the cinema and theatre thanks to fake press cards . . . pour la cause. Surely Donald had done his share of dirty work? Who had found a buyer for the manuscript in New York?

"It's true I was sent to New York, but not with stolen goods."

"What? So who sold it?"

"It wasn't sold. Catherine stepped in. I don't know what she told you, perhaps she didn't want to hurt your feelings. But after you left the thing was returned to the library."

"And you never bothered to tell me?" Mulder said. "What are you getting at?"

"Stop asking stupid questions."

"I was showing off. Not to Catherine, as it happens, because she wasn't interested in machos. It was you I wanted to impress."

Rising from his chair, Mulder caught sight of himself once more in the dark windowpane – none too steady on his feet, but respectable-looking. He made a little bow, as though saluting himself, and said, "Dumbo."

A sunbeam crept across the bed. Two unshaven men eyed each other in disbelief. The wind ruffled their hair. They had fallen asleep with the curtains open and the windows flung wide, hadn't even bothered to take their clothes off. Mulder lay crumpled up against Donald's shoulder. But the harmony was short-lived. A text message beeped, a belated note from Winston: *"Trouble in the village. 78 fishers arrested."*

"Let's go back," Mulder said during breakfast.

"I thought you wanted to exercise your memory?"

"That can wait. The fishermen will be needing your help."

"What, all seventy-eight of them? I'm not a lawyer – it's their affair. They have to get used to standing up for themselves. The most I can do is get in touch with *Die Burger*."

Mulder looked out at the dark clouds over the hills. "It gets so dismal here when it rains. The weather's bound to be better on the coast."

"Don't worry, I won't leave those fishermen in the lurch. I don't walk away from problems." Donald scalped his boiled egg with surgical precision. "And you're not walking away either. We will finish what we started."

*

Outside, in the parking lot, the cottage proprietor was surveying the vineyard through a pair of binoculars. "They've been at it again," he said, pointing to the disturbed soil. Several vines were missing. It was the third time this had happened. Thieves in the night? No, what would they do with stolen vines? It was a sign of anger, possibly jealousy. Or boredom. "Ten years of patience destroyed in a single night."

They drove into the hills. "The coast is to the right," Mulder said. Donald turned left.

The fields stretched away on either side, dark and steamy, with vines undulating row upon row. Perfectly maintained roads, tidy verges. This was the Cape as many whites liked to see it: a European Cape, a showcase of their own civilisation. The Cape of the La Bri winery, the Dieu Donné, the Domaine d'Ivoire . . . Africa had been ploughed under. No squalor here, no beggars leaping uninvited to wash your windscreen at traffic lights. Fortune-hunters, though, were thick on the ground according to Donald: Russians, Japanese, bonus boys from London, a German stock market speculator and a self-styled Italian count. Since the changeover the new rich had been buying up the old estates with hard cash.

"Are you making a detour?" Mulder said.

Donald passed him the map. "You know the way around here better than I do."

The map remained folded.

They marvelled at the ostentatious entrance gates. Old vineyards had been amalgamated and given new names. Donald pulled up, seized the map and spread it out.

"What are you looking for?"

"What do you think? A house on a hill, that's what. White, wasn't it?"

"Enough of the sarcasm, if you don't mind. I do remember it, honestly."

Donald turned off the main road onto an uphill track and engaged the 4x4. Grit spurted up. He lowered the windows. "So good to feel the cool breeze on your face."

A different season was impinging on Mulder's conscience, a summer of weeks without rain.

"Does it look familiar?" Donald said. "Is this the right direction?"

This was the track he must have gone up on the motorbike a dozen times, to the house where Catherine was born. Unbeknown to her father, the darling daughter had made Die Hugenoot a postal address for the resistance. A famed wine estate far removed from the city and rebellion serving as an address for subversive printed matter – unthinkable even to the security police. There was nothing unusual about a wine grower receiving mail from overseas. For a long dry summer Marten was to call there every fortnight to collect an envelope. He had got to know her parents, to whom Catherine's friends were their friends, especially Marten, the fair-haired charming student from Europe.

It was Marten acting the hero in those days, not Mulder. God, how scared he'd been riding down the hill with one of those clammy envelopes stuffed under his shirt. Scared of being stopped by traffic police, scared of an accident, scared to death in his rented room for as long as he was still in possession of the envelope. First he had to decipher the code to find out where the drop was, which was usually in the university library, tucked away in a pile of church journals in the reading room. Sometimes he was instructed to go to the harbour. He prayed that he wouldn't do the unthinkable one day – steam it open and read the contents. His fear held him back. The same fear that inspired the actor in him when, having accomplished his mission, he joined the soldiers on leave at the boarding house in a light-hearted round of beer. Fear was his most faithful companion during that summer.

———

Mulder brushed the dust from his shirt. "Where do you think Catherine is now?"

"Back in Paris, so they say."

"I've been looking for her all over the place. When I moved back to Paris I quite often thought I saw her at a pavement café, and I'd go over and talk to whoever it was. Sometimes I even wanted it to be someone else, but no-one smelled like her. She smelled of nothing, you know, nothing at all."

———

The Présence Africaine bookshop also became a favourite haunt for Mulder the student from Amsterdam. He would call there each time he hitchhiked to Paris, not because of the African connection, but because of Catherine. It was several months before he ran into her.

How was the dog getting on?

"*O, ce pauvre chien . . .*" She had almost forgotten about it; the vet had said there was nothing he could do to save the poor animal. Had Marten been there when the accident happened? Indeed he had, and he had read *Cry, the Beloved Country* straight after that. Great book.

They got talking. She took him for a drive. He dined with her friends: refugees, exiles, writers, publishers, artists. Black, white, Chinese, Indian. Nobody was a foreigner, because they all were. By the end of the first week she had found him a place to stay with an

Irish priest living with a black woman from Lesotho. It became his springboard to Paris.

At home in Amsterdam he explored the nightlife, but in Paris the nights took on a new meaning. Catherine's friends spoke five languages, switching from one to the other with ease. They debated the merits of philosophers, they argued about books, they discussed Biafra and Vietnam. Their stamping ground was a café near the rue Faubourg Saint-Antoine. It was where the members of a new world order held their meetings, chaired by Poubelle (who eschewed showers and clean clothes as being bourgeois), with the assistance of Phare, a pretty anarchist with red hair. They were an exalted bunch, harbouring grandiose conspiracy theories, and yet he had learned a lot from them: they had widened his world and dismantled his social conditioning. It was possible to live in two or three countries at once, even if you weren't rich, and in different cultures. One moment velvet, sandpaper the next. Your role was determined by the setting. If you weren't sure who you were, you could be try being someone else for a while. Catherine encouraged him in this.

He roamed Paris on his own, too, and sometimes woke up in different embraces. He wasn't particular, and after such a night he would feel all the more need for beauty and purity, for spiritual upliftment and transcendence – those highbrow words again, how he loved them then. He thought it might be time for him to take a stand himself, perform some act of commitment. But he was still at the reconnaissance stage. Only by getting lost would you find your way, only by making mistakes can you learn. It was not so much about having a goal, that was for people who knew where they wanted to end up; what he sought was direction. He was a traveller, a young man in transit.

But he always went back to Catherine. He had to escape from her now and then, or she from him – they were faithful in their infidelity. After hanging out together for several days she would suddenly be gone. Until he saw her again, a day later, or a week, in their café, or on a terrace feasting on an éclair, with a smile good enough to eat. In high spirits. Oh, the lightness of her being! What a woman, what times they'd had . . . He was twenty-four and happy (he thought later). Yes, she had reeled him in.

––––––––

"Did you find that godforsaken Hugenoot estate on the topographic map?" Mulder asked.

"The names of the old vineyards aren't indicated, but I think I know where it is."

"I don't need to see the place."

"But I do. It was me who addressed the envelopes and wrote the codes under the postage stamps. I wouldn't mind seeing where Catherine grew up."

A pickup truck came towards them. In the back sat two youths holding rifles. The wing mirrors knocked together when the two vehicles crossed paths. Donald struck up a conversation with the driver, who said they were going after vandals. Mulder stared ahead.

The vineyards extended over the hills, the sun-facing slopes showing a green flush of new growth. Donald praised the view. "You know every inch of this road and there you are, wrapped up in the past, remembering all the names and the most trivial details, and yet you've gone all quiet. What's the matter with you? Isn't Catherine worth the effort?"

"Some things are ruined by talking about them."

"She was arrested in front of her parents, for God's sake. It was the day after you left. Betrayed."

"Yes, I know."

"She got five years for treason! And that doesn't bother you?"

"Why do you think I broke with Fraternité? The whole set-up leaked like a sieve."

Donald stopped the car. Pee stop.

"You had an affair with her," Donald said, standing wide-legged staring into the distance.

"We wrote to each other, even in South Africa," Mulder replied defiantly. "Against the rules, I know. She mentioned that she'd seen you."

"Oh, that. I stayed with her a few times. I stayed with all sorts of girlfriends, so I could rent out my room. My pa had stopped my allowance."

Mulder did not pursue the subject.

They peed on the dusty ground. Mulder's trouser legs got spattered by a few pellets of earth, but to him it felt like a mud bath. Strange how a stain could grow and shrink in the mind. You could be painfully aware of it, or you could ignore it. Pain or no pain. It was the same with memories. His love for Catherine had only grown – even if he hadn't been faithful – but the pain at her arrest had gone into hiding. Plenty of experiences had been smothered by him in this way, or else trivialised or inflated, but on this trip the true proportions imposed themselves, and more misfortunes came up than he had expected . . .

As he watered the land, Mulder saw the grapes ripen in the vineyards, he saw the curly gables of the big house – old Cape Dutch style, dazzling white. He saw Marten tearing up the hill, taking the last stretch in first gear, saw him parking the motorbike at the back of the house, where a servant promptly offered him a glass of ice-cold water and brushed the dust from his clothes. Marten knew his way about the house, he patted the Karoo chairs, smoothed his hair in the reflection of shiny wooden cupboards and greeted a kneeling figure polishing the dark-red floor tiles.

The lady of the house, pink as a powder puff, received him in the drawing room. The envelope was waiting. She greeted him, beaming. "You'll never guess who's arrived in the country! Catherine!"

"She's in South Africa? Really?"

"Just for a week. She wanted to surprise us."

He was at pains to hide his bewilderment.

"Aren't you pleased?"

"Yes, yes, it's just so unexpected, that's all."

It was only three days since they had said goodbye at Cape Town airport. Why hadn't she said anything? Had something happened in the meantime? His hand shook; he spilt some coffee on his trousers. Questions raced through his mind, but all he asked was: "And when is she coming?"

"Any time now. She's on her way."

Heels tapped on the tiled floor. Catherine was acting the Parisienne. She wore a white trapeze dress edged with black – Courrèges from top to toe, down to the low-heeled white boots. The skirt was rather short by white South African standards, but the style as a whole was pronounced by her mother to be "completely Catherine".

He had not ever seen her looking like this before. So fashionable, with a silly smirk on her face. Still, his heart skipped a beat at the sight of her long legs. The same legs he had run the tip of his tongue along only a few days ago, from the soles of her feet up to where the hair began. And now he was given a cool peck on the cheek, as though she hardly knew him, the half-baked student from overseas who couldn't get by without his batch of newspapers from Europe.

Her father entered the room, felt hat in hand, smelling of vineyard. He embraced his daughter, lifted her off the floor and joked about her appearance: *o la la*, the very latest thing from Paris, eh, was that a good idea? Another guest appeared: "A friend from Pretoria." Meneer Treghardt wore a dark three-piece suit. Had Marten heard correctly? Treghardt . . . Karel Treghardt! This man had to be Donald's father. The Afrikaner leader addressing the crowd in the newspaper photograph. The man from the Justice Ministry, a friend of Catherine's father! He wasn't supposed to know this, was he? Or was it some kind of warning: was it something he needed to know?

Catherine and her mother were busy chatting. She gave him no sign whatsoever. Her father and the family friend reminisced about hunting parties; they touched on the political situation and the necessity of taking a hard line, but not for too long for fear of spoiling the atmosphere.

Mr Treghardt was curious to know how many South Africans were currently living in Paris.

The student from overseas had no idea.

No further questions were asked.

The sparkling wine went round. One glass and Marten said he had better be off; it was a long way to Stellenbosch. Catherine accompanied him outside to his motorbike, and as they went past the dining room he noted that the table was laid with four settings. He didn't understand, he demanded to know what was going on. "Later, later," she murmured. He tried to kiss her, but she pushed him away. The staff might be watching

She waved goodbye as he set off down the hill. Glancing back when he reached the gate he could see her still waving.

As he drove on, Marten soon felt there was something missing. The fear. The clammy sensation under his shirt. He had forgotten the envelope.

Sod it, he thought.

The following day there was a knock on the door of his room. A soldier held out a yellow envelope – delivered to the boarding-house that morning. The flap had been tampered with. The envelope felt suspiciously slim. He opened it nervously. It contained advertising leaflets.

That same evening Marten spat out his name and left the country as Mulder. Mission unaccomplished.

———

Their voices dropped. Dust clouds swirled in their wake.

"How many people knew about the Hugenoot address?" Mulder said.

"I did, and so did Duriez, as far as I know . . . They shot him dead on his doorstep."

Mulder hid his shock in a fit of coughing.

Donald pulled up by a gated driveway, leaving the engine running. They did not get out of the car. Up on the hill stood the Cape-style mansion, as shimmering white as ever. Mulder did not look up, he was staring at the gate. The name on it was new: Die Hugenoot was now called Doublecross Hill.

"Sick joke," Donald said.

The hilly wine country lay behind them, and after two days of rolling veld they approached the coast. The light changed, the green was shot through here and there with sand, birds skimmed low overhead. But the two men weren't paying attention to the scenery; they did not see the wind-flattened bushes. A strained silence had invaded the car. Mulder was mulling over his guilty memories.

Of course he had been overcome with grief. And anxiety. It had taken weeks for it to dawn on him that Catherine had been arrested. Back in Holland he was angry that he didn't hear from her. Letters to Die Hugenoot went unanswered, servants hung up on him when he phoned. He hitchhiked to Paris and had to summon his courage to call at the Irish priest's house, where he was shown a cutting from the *Cape Times*: "Bad year for Huguenots: family heiress arrested."

Where was Donald? The office kept by Duriez had been closed down. He went to Donald's lodgings and left a worried note behind. No reaction. He couldn't find the streets where they had done their training, each day in a different quarter. He recognised a metro station, a boulevard, but that was all. And people at the "global change" café seemed to have forgotten all about Catherine. He kept thinking he saw her: across the street, in the bus, or eating an éclair on a terrace. He had been utterly bewildered, and yet that was ages before his first stroke.

He had returned to Amsterdam feeling wretched. He phoned all the Treghardts in the Pretoria telephone directory. No-one could help him.

During the night he loved her, but there was resentment too. Why had he allowed himself to be strung along? He was anything but a hero. Far too self-centred. Why on earth had he thrown himself into a struggle that had nothing to do with him? Did he have any idea what it was like to be treated as a third-rate citizen? Had he received letter bombs? Had he been banished, spied on day and night? He had no need of a plastic surgeon to be able to start a new life. All it took was a new name.

Past blunders kept him awake. In the end there was only one thing left: the memory of love, magnified through self-recrimination.

The wind rose to gale force, tumbleweeds scudded over the tarmac, black clouds glowered on the horizon.

"The farmers must be burning the stubble." Donald slowed down and took the binoculars from the glovebox.

But that sudden chill in the air, the shivery sensation under their shirts, the ostriches stampeding in fright? No, it was not smoke, more like a cold storm blowing in from the sea. They put up the car windows.

Sheep were being driven into thorny enclosures. One of the ewes had just lambed, the umbilical cord trailed behind her. The lamb teetered on spindly legs; she tried to lick it clean, but the herdsman gave her a hard shove.

Pellets fell on the bonnet, thick and fast, and in no time the windscreen was covered in a film of viscous mush, too thick for the windscreen wipers. Mulder opened his window a chink. A hairy, slimy substance trickled inside. They had hit a swarm of bees in mid flight. Bees coming from the sea? Donald pulled over to the kerb and they got out of the car in consternation. The car buzzed with myriads of wings quivering on the bonnet. A sweet smell of dying bees.

"Have you ever seen this before?" Mulder stared in wonder at the insects in their death-throes.

Donald pointed to a flock of screeching seagulls. "They're fleeing from something."

The binoculars offered no explanation, but there was an ominous rumbling to be heard. Tractors? A helicopter? Donald tried to call the village. The phone rang out at the other end, but the connection kept falling away. His battery was low.

They scraped the muck off the windscreen and drove on slowly with the car windows opened just a little way, listening to the sounds of nature. Rounding a bend, they saw a lorry blocking the road. Donald rummaged under his steering wheel. Mulder heard the rip of Velcro: a pistol emerged. "Put it away!" he burst out. "You're not one of those loonies are you?"

Donald laid it down beside the handbrake and drove very slowly towards the lorry. Mulder took up the weapon: a memento of Paris. His fingers recognised the Beretta instantly. He ejected the magazine, pulled the slide back, and as he emptied the chamber into his hand was tempted to throw the lot out of the window, but then had second thoughts. The touch of cold steel was seductive. His right index finger caressed the trigger, he could feel Catherine's hand – a sensation he suppressed by jamming the barrel into the heel of his thumb. A hard kiss.

Donald nudged him with his elbow and honked insistently. Mulder stowed the pistol plus bullets resolutely in the glovebox. The lorry stayed put. Three men emerged from behind it, Boers armed with binoculars and rifles. They were to let no-one pass, on the orders of army and police. Everyone had been called up, there weren't enough men. Hadn't they heard the news about the storm flood? People had been swept out of their homes, stretches of duneland had crumbled away. After days of violent thunderstorms the ground couldn't take any more rain . . . and then there was the sea, the raging sea.

Half the fishing village was flooded. Three dead up till now, and nobody knew how many wounded, but the helicopters kept coming and going. Whirr, whirr, as if those poor sods hadn't been punished enough already.

Donald and Mulder stumbled over their questions, but the Boers had little more to tell. News was slow. Lines were down, telegraph poles snapped in two and stretches of tarmac washed away. And there was mud, mud everywhere, a metre deep in places. A subterranean stream had apparently been laid bare in the nature reserve. Water brought to the surface by water – a riddle, a cruel riddle. Only the road to Distriksdorp was still intact.

Donald asked to borrow a phone, as his own had given up. He keyed in all the numbers his thumb could recall, but without success. They turned back and took the road to Distriksdorp.

Darkness fell, a sea eagle winged ahead of them. Mulder asked where Hendrik's detox clinic was. Donald replied that it was far from the coast, an old hospital on the Cape plains. Charmein was not mentioned. Nor was there any mention of the village, but a telling sign was the line of army trucks with mechanical diggers coming from the opposite direction.

Cigarettes glowed in the dark at the side of the road: people trying to hitch a ride. As they drove past the shopping mall they saw a straggle of micro-skirted girls. The bullets rattled in the glovebox. Mulder fed them back into the Beretta. At a sign saying HOSPITAAL Donald turned onto an uphill road. There was no point in driving on and on, they decided. Maybe they should call at the first aid post, there was bound to be more information there.

Charmein lay in a hospital bed, moaning softly. She was hooked up to an intravenous drip, looking very pale. The air smelled strongly of bandages and plaster of Paris. The ward was crowded; nurses flurried about. Donald had already discovered the state she was in on arrival: a double fracture of the leg, a shattered knee, and a gash in her forehead. He kissed her on the cheek. Mulder contented himself with a feeble handshake. They had to remain standing at the foot of the bed – two male visitors! – or people would gossip. Her voice was weak, but after a sip of water she gathered enough strength to ask after Hendrik. Had they had any news?

"They're taking good care of him," Mulder said. He sounded optimistic.

But where was he? Where?

"We're going to visit him tomorrow," Donald said, taking the only available chair and placing it at the side of her bed so he could feel her pulse and peer into her eyes for signs of concussion. Charmein submitted meekly to his examination. Mulder couldn't bear to watch, and wandered off past the other beds, all of which were occupied by women, mostly with broken bones. Their daughters milled around them. "Is this a women's ward?" he asked a passing nurse. No, it was not, but all the fishermen had been rounded up and taken away by the police a few hours before the storm broke, so only

143

women had been injured. There had been some kind of uprising.

Mulder made his way back to Charmein's bed. He watched as Donald sounded her back. "You've been lucky," he said.

She smiled wanly. "I was saved by my bed." According to the rescue team, the roof of her house had been lifted off by the rising water, and she must have floated away still asleep in her bed surrounded by toy pandas. They had found her a hundred metres from her home, stranded in the base of a pylon. She had no memory whatsoever of what had happened.

Her face clouded again. But what about Hendrik? Where had they found him then?

Well, he was at the detox clinic, wasn't he?

No, he wasn't: he had run away, turned up on her doorstep the afternoon before the storm.

Donald swore under his breath. "So now you tell me! It's only supposed to be a first-rate clinic."

Charmein protested that she had tried to call Donald several times, but he never answered. She had been so desperate that in the end she had slipped the sedative pills into Hendrik's Coca-Cola, so as to keep him indoors. The briefcase was no longer an issue: the police had arrested dozens of fishermen, and one after the other had confessed.

She blinked away her tears. It was all her fault. When Hendrik woke up he had threatened her with a chair, demanding money to go into town. She had lashed out at him, striking his broken arm, and then he had run off yelling blue murder.

Donald plumped up her pillows. "Perhaps he's gone off with his friends, and doesn't know about the flood."

"He never forgave me for moving here from Cape Town, but I did it for his sake. I wanted him to grow up in a safe environment."

"He probably attracted less attention in the city, whereas he's an incomer in the village because of his Chinese dad."

"But he liked being noticed," Donald said. "Remember his Jackie Chan act on the beach?"

Charmein nodded. "He was wearing his pink sneakers when he left . . . baie smart." He might be looking for her even now, or he might be ringing at Donald's gate. The sea had become calmer, she had been told, the water was receding fast. They were to look out for his pink sneakers, his pride and joy.

"My rotten son, my damn son," whimpered Charmein. "Oh my Lord, my Lord." She wanted to fold her hands in prayer, but got no further than a single clenched fist.

It was pitch-dark when they left the hospital, with heavy clouds blanketing the stars. The road to the coast was closed off, as the army allowed vehicles to pass only during daylight. A second-rate hotel still had some rooms available – highly priced on account of the emergency. While Donald tried to reach Winston by landline, Mulder leafed through the old newspapers lying around in the lobby.

The flood had made the headlines: "FISHERWOMEN DROWN IN OWN HOME" and "CASUALTIES ONLY AMONG THE POOR". One paper described the course of the spring tide, the next its impact on the population – shock and awe were white, death was coloured. But all agreed on the weather: class 4 storms, with clouds like "fists of God". And the red flag in the harbour, with the waves crashing over the cold store within the hour. The worst disaster in living memory: power lines down, waterlogged yards, paths washed away, ground caving in, pipes broken in pieces.

A mother was pictured on the front pages holding a crumpled

snapshot of three smiling children: Jefta, Jonas and Jozef. She had climbed up a tree with her little boys, and had sat on the branches for hours singing psalms, while the water rose and rose. "Then the tree began to shake from the debris crashing against the trunk, and it toppled over. I could only hang on to two of my little ones. Our firstborn lost his grip."

A blind woman owed her life to her freezer. She had lifted the lid and settled down among the frozen fish, after which she had "floated around for hours". Rescue workers were interviewed, heroes who had pulled children out of a mud-filled hollow in the dunes. Even the poachers were on their best behaviour, ferrying the injured to the main road in their buggies. Solidarity had prevailed.

A soldier told the *Daily Sun*, "All the bodies were naked; now and then we would see an arm, a leg or a rump sticking out of the wreckage." There was a picture of an infant, its rosy, gaping little mouth filled with mud. Yes indeed, the *Daily Sun* sees everything.

Die Burger quoted the mayor as saying there had been subversive forces at play, not just the wind and the sea, but also wicked rebellion against the rule of law. The villagers had been incited not to pay their sewage tax, which was why the water could not drain away as it should. A news item that Mulder quickly laid aside.

The following day Donald and Mulder set off again early. The sun shone, the puddles were drying up and the clouds were thinning. The sand drifts covering the road surface in places were already dimpled with hoof prints. Dainty, ladylike. Nature seemed at peace once more, with ostriches running alongside the car and baboons begging at the roadside. The returning gulls flew ahead of them. Mulder was the first to catch the scent of the sea. Donald pointed to the biggest roof among the sand-dunes – his house, intact as far as they could tell. The under-village was a dark dip on the horizon. The road to the harbour was covered over in mud, and blocked to civilian traffic. They took the high track. The rain had gouged out ravines in the verges and laid bare the foundations of boundary walls, but the villas stood unshaken in their concrete robustness. Donald could not conceal his relief, but catching sight of his gate he slammed his horn in shock. His wall was streaked with tar, and the garage door refused to rise automatically. He parked the car opposite the gate and checked the lock and the receiver: fat globules of resin leaking from both. Tar and resin on the gate, too. The brass doorbell had gone. Forcing the locks was impossible. They would have to go over the wall. Mulder gave him a leg up; Donald reached for the top, cutting his fingers on a shard of glass, and dropped back. He swore and tied his handkerchief around his hand. They threw pebbles over the wall onto the terrace. No reaction. Where were the dogs, why weren't they barking? Where was Winston?

Donald ran over to the reinforced gates across the road, rang the neighbours' bell, rattled the handle, shouted into the intercom. A croaky voice replied that the mister and missus were out. Mulder stood about, watching, then climbed a nearby dune to take a look at his holiday home. The thatched roof was in shreds, he didn't need binoculars to see that. But he was in no hurry to go there. First they had to find Hendrik, and Winston, and the dogs. He went back down the dune, glancing over his shoulder a few times. Donald was standing in the middle of the road, licking the blood from the palm of his hand. Only then did they realise what it said on the boundary wall. The tar formed a dripping FOK OF.

They went down to the harbour. The boats had gone, as had the fried squid stall, and beyond, between the cottages, ran a river of mud, glistening in the morning sun. Two vultures flew overhead. The hotel had weathered the storm undamaged, aside from some broken flagpoles. The military and officials were quartered there, the parking lot was filled with army trucks. The no-man's-land between the upper dunes and the under-village was occupied by rescue workers, with tents for the homeless and a bus serving as a makeshift kitchen.

Donald and Mulder followed the trail left by the flood down to the worst-hit area, where Charmein and Hendrik lived. Mulder's shoes got stuck in the mud – his boots lay useless in his suitcase. His eyes felt stuck, too, to a dead dog, a teacup with a fancy handle, unscathed, then to the occasional shoe, which was never a pink sneaker. The force of the tide had shattered windows, demolished walls, set adrift sheets of corrugated iron. A lamppost had snapped in two, dislodged roofs lay all around. At the lowest point the army had roped off an improvised footbridge; rescue workers bustled about.

They asked after Hendrik.

Hendrik? Well, a boy had been brought in yesterday, in total shock after spending a whole day on a roof with a snake for company.

Was his right arm in plaster by any chance? Did he look a bit Chinese?

No, just sullen. A mere child. His mother was missing. And not long ago the body of a girl had surfaced, still clutching her mobile as she was overtaken by the mud. But a Chinese with his arm in plaster? No.

They wanted to go and search for Hendrik themselves, but were stopped by a man in an orange overall. Donald said he was a doctor, but was told that medical volunteers had to apply at the hotel. It was up to the mayor to give out permits.

"Not up to the rescue workers then?" Mulder said in surprise.

"No, the mayor," the man sneered.

They turned around and made their way to the higher, less poverty-stricken part of the under-village, where the buildings were still standing. People were sweeping the mud out of their homes, the smell of cesspits was overpowering. Young girls carried jerrycans of water; there was no pressure in the taps. Children, still numbed by recent horror, hovered in doorways. Washing was hung out to dry, fires were being lit in the yards. Life was back on its noisy track, but fell silent as Donald and Mulder drew near. Men shut their doors, women ducked away behind flapping sheets people who knew Donald, people he had seen in his study, people for whom he had written letters.

149

Mulder grew increasingly dispirited. An oyster-seller tried to catch his eye. He waved. She smiled briefly, then ducked away like the rest. Donald wanted to find Winston's house, but had no idea where to look. Strange, considering the old man had been working for him for such a long time. But it couldn't be helped, it was the way things were: coloureds made their way up the dunes in numbers, but rarely did whites come down.

A male nurse from outside the village took them to the prayer hall, where a first aid post had been set up. Who knows, Hendrik or Winston might have been seen there. It was where all casualties, dead or alive, were registered. Besides, they would have records establishing who among the seriously injured had been transferred to hospitals inland.

A crowd had gathered by the entrance, anxious for news of missing family members. A list was passed around, names were spelled out. Three young victims had not yet been identified, a girl aged four or five with a mole on her lower back (lifted from a gutter), a toddler with an earring (swept away under the eyes of a fisher's wife) and a three-week-old baby (the baby that had made the front pages). "The mud is cruel," a woman said. With bowed heads, Donald and Mulder awaited their turn to ask for information.

In the forecourt stood wheelbarrows filled with clothes and shoes, all of them caked with mud. Mulder fished out a few garments and rummaged among the shoes. No pink.

Rescue workers pressed forward: yet another child had been found. The body was in the tent behind the prayer hall. Where was the woman responsible for listing the names of the dead? Someone volunteered to go and fetch the tannie in charge. A large woman appeared, flushed with excitement: Stienie, in white trousers and a shirt with press-studs. Mulder held out his arms. She was delighted to see him: "Where have you been? Why didn't you leave a message?" She kissed him on the lips, ignoring Donald. "I'm so sorry about your roof. If only we'd had a key."

Mulder interrupted her, asking after Hendrik. Youngster, arm in plaster, Chinese features . . .

"At the back," she whispered. "I'll join you in a minute."

The colour drained from Donald's face. At the back was the tent where the dead were lined up.

They waited in mute dismay, shoulder to shoulder, each thinking of the Hendrik they had come to know. "He could have gone so far," Donald said. "If only I'd been stricter with him."

Mulder pictured the youngster in his pink sneakers, defiant, vain about his looks, much like himself at that age, wearing his father's tropical canvas boots with rust around the eyelets and a bloodstain on the heel. A war hero with knobs on.

Stienie returned with her list. "Who exactly are you looking for?"

"The tik-head we gave a lift to," Mulder said.

"Oh, that beggar." She tossed her head impatiently. "You're not still fussing about him are you? In any case, he hasn't been found."

And Winston?

The key-man? What was his surname?

They didn't know.

Stienie ran her finger down a list of names. She had cut her nails, in keeping with her new nursing status. No, nobody called Winston.

So why had she told them to wait by the lugubrious tent at the back?

"Not a good idea for you to stand over there among the grieving families. There's too much tension in the village as it is." She indicated the dunes with a wave of the hand. "We had waves sloshing into our pool and our lawn was covered in sand, but we stayed indoors and sat by the fire. Down here the ground caved in under their feet. Because of the lack of a proper sewage system. At least that's what the mayor says."

Donald kicked at the mud.

"Yes, he's got some cheek," Stienie said. "Yesterday he laid claim to our dunes. He was on the radio. It is their land, he said. Land belonging to the first people."

"What about you, then?" Donald said. "Do they accept you being here?"

"I have to tread very carefully, but I was the first to come here and offer to help, even before the army or the police. I was wearing my nursing outfit." She drew in her stomach. "If I don't bend over too much it still sort of fits."

The neighbours had said she was mad, but what really drove her mad was sitting at home doing nothing. "I was so upset I couldn't sleep. I just had to go and see for myself." She had come armed with iodine, alcohol and clean sheets. Kobus, her husband, had followed her to the under-village with a reel of nylon fishing thread, so she could stitch up small wounds if need be. She gave Donald a challenging look. She had not waited for a yes or no from the authorities, not she. She had taken a broom and swept the prayer hall in person. After some persuasion she had got the hotel manager to part with a few beds. And so now here she was, in charge of her first aid post, cleaning the mud from people's eyes and ears, disinfecting the wounds of skollies she had been cursing only a week before. Stienie distributed bandages and kindness.

The fishers had taken to calling her Tannie.

Donald offered his assistance.

Stienie looked embarrassed. "Things are a bit too difficult now." Her nose-bump quivered.

Donald was incensed. It was imperative he should see the mayor. Immediately. A question of honour. The honour of a man who cared deeply about the fishing community, the honour of a doctor, of a freedom fighter. He was going straight to the hotel, having charged Mulder with continuing the search for Hendrik and Winston. "And the dogs, too. Don't forget my dogs."

"Do you know Dirk?" Stienie said. A gangly fellow with skinny arms and legs was approaching the tent. His shoes were encrusted with mud. He was looking for his mother.

Mulder had seen him around the harbour. Dirk was a deaf-mute, his tongue lolled in his toothless mouth. In his youth he had been given a medicine that destroyed his teeth to the roots, according to the locals. His usually wide grin had gone, his lips were now pursed in sorrow. His mother's body lay in the tent.

"I am so sorry, Dirk," Stienie said kindly, "but at least your ma didn't suffer too much."

Dirk gave her a blank stare. He had already been told by several people about his mother's death, overtaken by a river of mud at some distance from her home. No-one could say what she was doing so far afield in the middle of the storm. He had been sitting at the kitchen table waiting for his supper. His neighbours had taken him to the tent, so that he could see for himself. Stienie took him by the arm and drew him inside.

The wind buffeted the canvas. Mulder hung around at the back of the tent, at a loss how to proceed. Where was he supposed to start looking for Hendrik and Winston? There were voices everywhere, young and old, dogs barking, the whole village was in an uproar. He wished he didn't feel so useless.

A girl was rinsing clothes under an improvised tap, her hands wringing out the mud. If only those hands were his! The girl stripped off her shirt and washed her breasts – flat shells. She gaped at him. He didn't know what to say.

Minutes passed in strained silence. Wide-eyed children peered round the corner, gulls balanced on the billowing canvas roof. Mulder looked about him, killing time.

Stienie emerged from the tent followed by Dirk, who seemed unmoved. He had finally understood, had even talked to his mother. "Well, sort of talked," Stienie said. Dirk went over to the tap to wash his hands. Stienie watched him with a tender look in her eyes.

Mulder saw Dirk taking what appeared to be a lump of mud from his trouser pocket. He held it under the tap, then popped the object into his mouth. He made chewing movements with his cheeks, in the course of which a few white teeth slid into view between his lips. His old mother's dentures. Dirk grinned. Her smile was a good fit.

The dogs had turned up. It was several hours before Donald told Mulder, for which he apologised with a grim chuckle: "They almost took me into custody." But first the good news: he had run into Winston at the hotel. Winston was fine, aside from having dropped his mobile in the mud, his house was still standing, and he had a lot of extra work as a result of the flood, like flushing the sand out of the water conduits. The dogs were staying with his grandson "on a ration of fish-heads". They were better off there than in the empty house without their master.

"And Hendrik?" Mulder said anxiously.

Not a trace. The police didn't know anything either. His description was being circulated.

They left the under-village and struck up the least soggy path to the parking lot. Donald was despondent. His face and clothes were bespattered with mud, as were Mulder's. Stienie had taken him to see the digging teams at work. Most of the water had drained away, no more bodies had been recovered. That left Hendrik as the only person still missing. Mulder stopped to ask a few tik-heads on the way. They demanded money in return for the vaguest of replies, such as that Hendrik might have hitched a ride in an army truck. Getting away from the place had never been so easy.

"I'm not allowed to leave for the time being," Donald said wearily. The police had questioned him at length, and they wanted him to be available as a witness. The mayor had brought charges against the people who had refused to pay their sewage tax. Donald scratched the two-day-old stubble on his chin. He looked haggard.

"Did you manage to speak to him?"

"No, his lordship was too busy holding meetings. But the bar was rife with gossip. Naturally, the council's not in the least to blame. The party . . ." His eyes glanced to his side. Keeping up with them was an old fisherman, nodding his head in mimed agreement. "What do you want?" he asked.

"A coat to keep my son warm."

"In this weather?" Donald looked up at the clear blue sky. "It's spring, man, too hot for coats."

"He's very, very cold," the man persisted, tugging at Mulder's sleeve. "A coat like this would be just right for him."

"Go away," Donald said.

"My son is dead. His body is blue with cold. I want him to be warm in his grave."

Mulder took off his wool jacket. It was part of his travel wardrobe, intended for chilly hilltops and evenings in unheated hotels. But the weather was already warmer than summer in Europe.

"Don't give it to him," Donald growled.

The man held out both hands.

Donald seized Mulder's arm. "Go on, keep walking. This is probably not the best time for distributing largesse. I'd have preferred to break the news to you more gently, but I'm afraid your roof has collapsed. Not only that, the rest of your house has suffered a fair amount of damage too. All your clothes will be soaking wet."

Mulder handed over his jacket. "For your son," he said.

The fisherman hurried away.

Donald snorted disapprovingly. "That's how you create beggars."

The locks were replaced that same afternoon. Winston had found some spare ones at the hotel, as well as a can of paint to cover the tarred graffiti. He had got hold of the brass bell for the gate in the parking lot, where a small market had sprung up in "washed-up goods". Donald was not amused. Not until all the opening and closing devices were functioning properly did Winston fetch the dogs. They cowered, and their breath smelt of fish. He also brought a tarpaulin for Mulder's roof. From a distance the roof didn't look too bad, but when the three of them went over to check they found there was very little they could do. Clumps of sodden thatch were sagging onto the exposed ceilings, the wet had seeped in behind the windows, baboons had done the rest. Bed, sofa and cupboards were steaming in the heat.

156

They went from room to room taking stock of the damage. Winston patted the damp walls, saying he had played in this very house as a child, when the dominee – "he was one of us" – was living there. Donald was somewhat taken aback by the new electrified wire on top of the neighbours' walls: four evil lines high, glittering in the sun. "How brave we all are," he murmured. Mulder paused in front of the wardrobe to sniff at his trousers and shirts: monkey poo and straw. The light wasn't working, the electrical sockets dangled from the walls. No trace of sugar ants. All eaten up, Winston said. The bathroom smelled dank and mouldy. The writing on the card tucked in the mirror to remind him of the pen-pal-seeking prisoner was barely legible. The washing machine, however, proved itself a veritable strongbox: the laptop emerged quite dry from the drum.

The Living Shores of Southern Africa still lay on the windowsill, swollen to three times its thickness with moisture. Mulder opened the window and inhaled deeply, by way of farewell to his rented view. He was never one to take photographs, as his memory would suffice (so he believed in the old days), but this time he wasn't so sure he wanted the scene to be imprinted on his mind: a harbour that was no longer a harbour, a slipway submerged in wreckage and mud, not a single fire burning in token of return to normality. No oyster-seller climbing the road up the dune.

He rang the estate agent, only to be informed that natural disasters were not covered by the insurance. Donald offered him the use of his guest room. Mulder had no choice but to accept. "I'll stay until Hendrik has been found."

He was to take only what was clean and in reasonable condition. His boots, brand-new still, his shoe trees, all his bottles and blister packs of pills, and Catherine's letters – thankfully undamaged and stuffed into in his bag when Donald's back was turned. Few clothes, as Winston would be taking charge of the laundry. "The Doctor and Meneer have the same size," he said appraisingly.

Mulder winced at such a degree of intimacy.

On the bedside table in the guestroom lay an Afrikaans Bible. It had a dedication on the flyleaf: *vir Faan, van jou Pa*. Mulder sat on the edge of the bed, leafing through the Old Testament. The glue creaked in the binding. From the kitchen came the inviting sound of glasses tinkling. Donald called out to him, but he did not answer. He was counting the pencil marks in Psalm 60, where it said: "Thou has made the earth to tremble, thou has broken it: heal the breaches thereof, for it shaketh."

Mulder shut the Bible quickly when Donald came to the door. The sparkling wine had been poured: a welcome drink. They drank their wine on the terrace and listened to the surf. The rumble of mechanical diggers could be heard in the distance. Evening fell as they reviewed the past days' events: the devastation, the casualties, the mud, the way people averted their eyes. But they both shied away from mentioning what was uppermost in their minds.

During supper they could prevaricate no longer. Where was Hendrik? How much damage had the tik done to his brain? They made plans for his future. "What if I get him to come and live with me?" Donald said.

"What if he goes to rack and ruin?" Mulder said. They had no answers.

The dogs barked all through the night. Unable to sleep, Mulder got up and crept through the house to the sound of dog claws tap-tapping over tiled floors. The thief in him hesitated in front of

158

cupboards and closed doors, but he did not lapse into past bad habits and did not touch anything.

The early morning walk began in the sand-filled hollow of the dunes. The old footpath was no longer distinguishable. They climbed steep slopes to pointed crests – the more exertion, the less need there was to talk. Nor did they pause for a drawing to be traced in the sand. There was nothing to explain.

No-one came to the gate during that morning. The letterbox remained empty, but for a silent token of protest: a clump of seaweed. The telephone did not ring. They drank strong coffee and listened to the voices out in the road. The atmosphere was leaden. Then Donald withdrew to his study. Mulder wished he could leave, but decided that would be cowardly. From now on it would be Hendrik keeping them together.

Donald topped up the glasses. His hands shook.

Mulder said, "How interesting."

The Major told them to call him Wessie. They were among themselves now, after all.

"I balance on the edge," Wessie said. "Oh, you can beat about the bush as much as you like, but the fact of the matter is that we now have illiterates occupying high posts. I waver between white and black. There's no other way in a rainbow nation." That was why he had been obliged to take Donald in for questioning. "To appease the mayor." All for show. A balancing act.

Mulder had put the Major in a talkative mood.

Donald grew impatient. "So what's the situation with Hendrik?"

Wessie drew his notebook from his inside pocket and flipped through it for a fresh page. "Why all this interest in the boy? You were concerned about him before, I know."

"I've managed to get him a study grant."

"His mother is a prostitute."

"Not anymore," Donald said fiercely.

"Ah, because of her broken bones?" Wessie suppressed a chuckle with a cough and scribbled in his notebook.

"What difference does it make, anyway," Mulder said. "We're concerned about the boy, and his talents lie in other areas."

Wessie jerked his head up. "Talents? Our colleagues in Cape Town plucked him from a drug house. He was out of his mind, had to cool off in a police cell. Sat there banging his head against the wall for hours. A talent for self-destruction, yes." He leafed through his notes. "It says here that he was break-dancing in his cell. Is that what you mean? Performing for a sniff of tik." Only the strictest discipline could save that kid. A stint in Boystown correctional facility would do him good.

"It would make him worse," Donald sneered. "He'd only learn a lot more bad stuff there. I'll get him to kick the habit here, in my house. *I'll* teach him discipline."

This was grist to the Major's mill. "Now you're talking! Like a true Treghardt, like a man of his word. You're a son of old Karel Treghart's, aren't you?"

Donald gave a stiff nod.

"Fine fellow, your pa. Admired by all the top people – the old guard, I mean." Wessie was sorry not to have met him. He had wanted to ask before whether Donald was a relation, but that wouldn't have been right during a police inquiry. Now was different. "You must have some pretty good memories of him, eh?"

Mulder saw the son cringing with shame for the father, yet also the father in the son, the patriarch of Die Hugenoot – amiable enough but imprisoned in a three-piece black suit. "Yes Donald, what was your father like?"

"Like an oak," he said coolly. (Angrily in Mulder's perception.) "And nothing much grows under a big spreading tree."

"Now that's a bit harsh," Wessie protested. "He was a man of granite, an example we all looked up to. That was back in the old days, when we all knew where we stood."

The tonic water had become tepid again, the sun crept over the terrace. They shifted their chairs into the shade. Donald sat back, withdrawing from the conversation.

The Major had a few points he still needed to discuss: medication, liability, permission from the mother, type of schooling and, last but not least, religious instruction. Donald would promise to take the boy to church, wouldn't he?

Weary of the Major, Donald said yes to everything. Mulder would also be acting as guarantor. "Money isn't a problem."

Wessie did not leave until another hour had passed. The dogs pranced about on the terrace.

Donald spent the rest of the day in his study and was not to be disturbed. "Not another word. I won't listen to another word on the subject." He made himself a quick sandwich in the kitchen, but ate it alone. He drank alone, too – at least two bottles.

Mulder, settled on the sofa with the dogs, heard Donald shouting down the phone. "*Mais non, Sarah! Non!*" The line to Paris was not a good one. He went outside to gaze at the sea, which he could see little of in the dark, and thought of his father, a man in uniform.

———

He saw his father naked, through the eyes of a child. Nobody else's father had so many scars: the gash between the shoulder blades from a burst of shrapnel (friendly fire), the dent in the shin from a booby trap (didn't go off) and the nick in the collarbone from a bullet, which ached in stormy weather. Adventures a mere boy could not compete with. The following summer his poor father was dead. All he left was a trunk filled with clothes, shoes and a tin containing medals. Treasures to be sniffed, stroked and listened to, for each had a story to tell. Or he would make one up. At the bottom of the trunk lay a knife with a long thin blade, which his father had somehow managed to hang on to throughout the war. His "art knife", he called it. He used it to sharpen his pencils, and he owed his life to it in the prison camp, where he drew portraits in exchange for food and to gain favours from guards who fancied themselves. Years later some old army chums of his father's had told a different story – it was a murder weapon. He had used it to stab a prisoner to death, someone who had snitched on his comrades to the camp commander for a morsel of meat. When the prisoner he shared his bunk with was also betrayed – he ended up facing a firing squad – old man Mulder had flung away his sketch pad and lunged at the traitor with his knife, stabbing him to the heart. He became the hero of the camp. Nobody had expected this from the gentle artist. The dead body was smuggled out; his fellow inmates stood by him. The word "amok" clung to that knife. Murderous frenzy. A knife that had grown weightier with time, a knife to show the children later on, so the old army chums said. But Mulder had thrown it in the dustbin, and in so doing severed his father from his life (or so he thought). Severed an entire line of descendants. To stop the insanity, the frenzy. And now suddenly he felt a sense of loss.

Shortly after sunrise Donald knocked on the guestroom door: would Mulder mind taking the dogs for their walk, so he could have a lie-in? His hangover was killing him.

Not a cloud in the sky, the air smelt salty, and there were fires burning once more in the under-village – early-morning cooking fires. The dogs bounded up the dune. Mulder trudged after them, glancing over his shoulder at regular intervals. Since their return from the wine country he had given the under-village a wide berth He missed the view from his window, the bustle, the women, the children, even the skollies. The expanse of mud down below had dried out, the mechanical diggers and army trucks had all gone. He thought of Stienie, and felt bad about not having contacted her. Or perhaps it was Donald he felt bad about, Donald the doctor who had allowed his offer of assistance to be dismissed out of hand.

The storm had blown the top layer of sand off the uphill path, laying bare a variety of old shells – oyster, nautilus and perlemoen – with mother-of-pearl gleaming in the morning sunlight. Mulder was sweating profusely, his eyes stung, he needed to sit down for a breather. An old crone caught up with him.

"Morning, Meneer."

"Morning, Mevrouw." Mulder recognised her, stood up and asked after her family.

Oh, did Meneer remember Riempie by any chance? Riempie her grandson, wayward child, forever drifting around, preferring to sleep in a boat rather than at home? Riempie was dead, swallowed up by the sea. Only his trousers had washed up on the beach.

"I'm so sorry." He wanted to give her a hug, but decided against it.

She set off again. "I'm going to see my father, I need to talk with him."

"Where does your father live?"

"In his grave. But he will listen to me." Her mother had buried him behind the dunes. In the year of The Law. In other words, illegally, just before they had all been forced to leave the high dune. It was sacred ground, a place you went to for solace when times were hard. "I go there to pray and weep, so my father and his ancestors will hear my voice and feel my tears. Perhaps they can put in a kind word with the sea. Riempie's body still hasn't washed ashore, and it's been more than a week now. We can't talk to him in the water. Riempie belongs in the earth. Riempie was never a fish."

Mulder wished her good luck.

During breakfast Donald hid behind the *Handbook of Neuro-surgery*.

Mulder poured him another cup of coffee, and was struck by the old-fashioned design of the book's cover. "Isn't all that out of date?"

Donald shrugged. In his student days it had already been established that the maturation of the prefrontal cortex accelerated during adolescence. The systems weren't properly aligned yet, with one lobe over-shouting the next, which could give rise to confusion and conflicting emotions. "You want to bungee jump, preferably without the elastic. We'll have to teach Hendrik the difference between taking unnecessary risks and having a good time." He showed Mulder the illustrations of giant slices of pickled walnut: the suprachiasmatic nucleus of the hypothalamus. He drew a diagram on a scrap of paper, muttering complicated jargon. Donald-speak.

Half of what he said was lost on Mulder. "How much damage has the tik already done, do you think?"

"We'll find out soon enough."

―――――

Hendrik arrived two days later than expected, in a state of utter exhaustion. He was barefoot, the pink sneakers having been stolen.

His breath smelt vile, a cut on his forehead was bleeding and his wrists were red and swollen from the tie wraps, which the policemen escorting him only snipped loose after Donald had signed the document accepting responsibility. They said the boy was a mess, banging his head against the partition in the police van throughout the journey – out of rage. They had even had to turn back to get the doctor to give him a shot of tranquilliser. They handed over the prescription. Donald crumpled it up under Hendrik's dull gaze. "We don't want that stuff. We will go about it in a different way."

Hendrik was to have the pink room, which had no door to the terrace. It was originally intended for the baby that never arrived, but for many years now it had served as a place to store old furniture. Hendrik was offered the choice of which chair to keep, but he wasn't interested; all he needed was a bed to sleep in. No chair then? No table to sit at and work? He didn't understand. How could you work sitting down? He said he was tired from the medication and lay down on the bed with his back to Mulder and Donald. He scratched the pink wallpaper. No, he didn't want water, just Coca-Cola and some crisps. When they did not oblige he spat on the floor.

"It's not a prison here," Donald said.

Mulder gave Hendrik his fountain pen. "Here, you can use it to write a letter to your mother."

Hendrik used it to scribble on the wall.

"What do we know about teenagers?" Mulder said.

"Well, seeing as it's a stage we both went through," Donald said, "we'll have our own experience to guide us." The main thing was to set a good example. "He needs us as role models."

They exchanged solemn promises about the boy's interest coming first at all times. They would not be too strict to start with. It was clear that Hendrik needed structure, but first they would give him some space to adjust. The next step would be the setting of limits, lovingly, not punitively, thereby enabling him to come to terms with the degree of his confinement. His eating habits had to change, too. No snacks, no soft drinks, but plenty of greens – raw, if possible – and three litres of green tea a day. Detoxification, purging the body of all harmful substances. Sweating was good, too. So was physical exertion. Floor-scrubbing and swimming, lots of swimming.

"Is sweating out an addiction really enough? Doesn't the trouble lie deeper down?" Mulder wondered aloud.

"We'll find some other kick for him," Donald said. "Some kind of risk he can live with and keep under control."

Underwater swimming perhaps? Ah yes, Mulder would teach him to dive.

Making plans. They were both good at that.

———

The second day Hendrik kept his mouth shut. Friendly gestures were counterproductive: he would not be touched, not patted on the shoulder, while a finger pointed at him was enough to make him bridle. Even an elbow coming close to his at the dinner table warranted a brusque shove.

Only the dogs were permitted to sniff him, tentatively at first, sneezing, wary of the poison emanating from his skin, and of the smell of tik on his hair. They licked him clean, to which he submitted with a shudder.

He kept his jaws clenched throughout dinner. They did not press him to eat. But he had to drink. Mulder tried to persuade him with words; Donald proposed force: twist his arm behind his back, hold his nose, jam a plastic cup between his teeth. Each insisted on the superiority of his approach, each vying for the boy's attention. Both were spat upon.

When Hendrik couldn't bear his hunger any longer he snatched food from the table and shared it with the dogs. He lay down with his head in their basket. The dogs let him be, even laid their paws around him. Hendrik hid his face in his fists.

Mulder sat at the kitchen table. "He's pretending to be a dog."

"Let's give him a bone then," Donald whispered in his ear.

"Wouldn't that be rather cruel?"

"He needs to realise that he's not fooling us with his behaviour. Let's see how far he's prepared to go."

Mulder strode to the fridge and threw three slices of ham into the basket. Hendrik threw his slice back. Offended.

"A human being after all," Mulder said.

Donald couldn't stand it any longer. He gave the basket a sharp kick.

The dogs barked and bared their teeth. They were protecting their young.

————

Speech was restored with the food. Broccoli and squash were on the menu, blanched in rosettes and slices.

"What's that?"

"Vegetables."

"I don't want any."

"You need vitamins."

"What are they?"

"Drugs, but healthy drugs."

Hendrik pushed the vegetables away. He demanded cola, but

was served tonic water instead. What was that? Too bitter. Down the drain with it. A banana? Bananas were for baboons. An apple? He pulled a face. Well alright then, pineapple slices from a tin, "the ones with a hole in the middle."

Donald ducked into the pantry and returned with a rusty tin of peaches. Hendrik devoured them in front of the window, knees wide apart. The sweetness had a calming effect. His first concession – they decided to wait a little before introducing the green tea.

———

Hendrik could not, would not, sit down. He had to be on his feet. Up and down the corridor, in and out of rooms, shower, lavatory, every metre stamped with a pair of Donald's sneakers that were two sizes too big. The crockery rattled in the cupboard. He slapped the walls with the flat of his hand, pressed his ear against them and listened, rolling his eyes. "Inspection!" He could hear voices in the house. Prison voices. And he knew what they were saying. Only he. And God.

After the inside walls it was the turn of the outside walls along the terrace. Tap, tap, every other brick. Mulder and Donald raised no objections to this, but neither did they let him out of their sight. Hendrik was not to escape. After the walls he began to hop from tile to tile. "Don't read, don't look," he muttered. It was a secret message. Now and then he made a big jump: he was dancing a crossword puzzle. From letter to word. When he bumped into Mulder by accident, he shrieked: "You were looking! You saw, I can tell by your eyes!" He lifted his arms and broke into long, tearless sobs.

"How weird is that?" Mulder said.

"Quite normal for a psychosis," Donald said.

"But he's playing games with us, can't you see? He knows what he's doing; there's method in it!"

Hendrik was listening, with one hand theatrically cupped to his ear.

The game took a different direction. Hendrik began to rail against Mulder: he was dangerous, his ears and eyes were everywhere. "Don't deny it! Don't deny it!" He ran to the kitchen and returned waving a knife. He was trembling all over. "You know! You all know!"

Donald spoke calm, soothing words to him. Mulder went inside, his hands shaking in his pockets.

"Everybody knows about my ma," Hendrik shouted after him. "My ma's a whore." The whole fokken dorp knew.

Donald asked for the knife; Hendrik handed it over.

Mulder returned with a bowl of tinned peaches. Hendrik slurped one up and spat it out at once. Another peach. More spitting and spraying. Yet another.

"That's enough," Donald said. "There's nothing wrong with those peaches."

Hendrik knocked the bowl over: "They're poisoned!" He stormed to the front room and threw himself face down on the sofa.

Having cleaned up the mess, Mulder and Donald sank onto their chairs and shared the remaining peaches between them. Exhausted from Hamlet-on-sea.

Winston stood in the hallway, more bent than usual. He had come to deliver a crate of Coca-Cola, directly from the hotel bar. Mulder had given Karneels a call, as he and Donald couldn't leave the house because of Hendrik. The dogs wagged their tails. Winston was agitated. He stank. He had been pelted with rotten fish by some skollies, punishment for running errands for the Doctor, he explained breathlessly. Moreover, the house was being watched.

The poachers were everywhere, the Doctor should be careful, the garage doors had been smeared with tar again, better for the Doctor and Meneer to stay home for a bit, keep a low profile.

Donald told him to calm down and handed him a glass of water. Mulder picked the fish scales off the collar of Winston's overall.

Hendrik hovered in the background.

Winston scowled. "What's he doing here?"

"Staying with us," Donald snapped.

People were talking. Winston was sorry, but he had heard some nasty gossip. "The poachers are angry with the Doctor."

Donald lost his patience. "What do you care what they say? They're scum."

Winston tittered nervously. "They say the Doctor isn't the boss round here."

"I am a democrat, and I do my democratic duty."

"The poachers say: 'We are Africa now.'"

"We?"

"I'm just telling you what they're saying. Not me, I would never say a word against the Doctor, but, er . . . a coloured boy living with two white men? The poachers don't like it. People don't do that in Africa."

"Thank you for sharing that with us, Winston. Dankie." Donald looked at Hendrik from the corner of his eye. Had he been following the conversation?

Winston held up a brand-new mobile. "If you need anything just give me a call." But he would not be doing deliveries during the day. "They mustn't see me coming here."

Donald paid for the Coca-Cola and counted the remaining notes in his wallet. He needed to go to the bank. Just as well Sarah had stocked up on groceries to last several weeks, but they were running low on treats. "You can bring me some tinned pineapple. Pineapple from Africa, go and tell that to the poachers."

———

Magazines held little interest for Hendrik, however richly illustrated. Donald had fetched a pile of back issues from the garage, to no avail. Hendrik had leafed through a *Paris Match*, a *Côté Sud*, an *Elle*, but his hands were unsteady and his fingers sweaty, so that the pages tore at the corners. He had discovered pictures of a different kind, moving pictures: the internet. Tap, tap, tap on the laptop, with a shaky left forefinger. He had never used a computer before, but learnt the basics from Mulder within the hour. Together they watched films on YouTube: angry rappers and Michael Jackson wearing a mask over his remodelled nose. They downloaded music (during which Hendrik found it impossible to sit still). A whole new experience, not least for Mulder, but between them they managed quite well.

Hendrik was eager for some computer games with gangsters and car chases – the poachers were always talking about them. But there was a hitch: you had to pay and the video kept breaking down. What did turn up on the screen was free porn. Was it alright for Hendrik to see that? Donald raised objections from the depths of his easy chair, to which Mulder countered that everybody came across it sooner or later. Better to watch it together than Hendrik getting hooked on it in secret. With flushed cheeks they watched three white girls dallying with a young black. (No sound, so as not to annoy Donald.) Hendrik said the girls were too skinny, and didn't smile enough.

"It's always better in your imagination," Mulder said.

They crept into a microscope, whooshed through an artery and listened to a beating heart (volume up). Donald came over to take a look as Google took them flying over Africa, with Mulder helping to steer across jungles and savannas. They zoomed in on the coast, then the fishing village and the dunes – peaceful images from before the flood. Donald's house leapt out at them. Seen from above it resembled a veritable fortress. Hendrik did not recognise it at first. "How do they do it?" "Who's flying the plane?" "Satellite photos? What are they?" He was too excited to wait for the answers. The computer had sent his brain into overdrive, and now he looked upon the world with the eye of God. Space was a mouse-click away from Africa. He skipped light-years, the present merging magically with the past as in the old fishermen's legends. Zoom, zoom! Hendrik was better at it than Mulder and Donald. And quicker. He gave a shout when they found themselves floating over Manhattan. They danced on the roof of a yellow cab, and flew from there to Taiwan, the island where his father was born. They zoomed in, and saw concrete bunkers along a desolate shore.

It was too much. Never before had he learnt such a lot in one day, Hendrik said. The immensity of it all! He slid down from his chair, worn out. He felt dizzy, needed to lie back on the cool tiled floor. "What do you call flying among the stars?"

"Space travel," Mulder said.

"And flying through a body?"

"Science."

Hendrik nodded gravely. "And when people clap for you?"

"Show business."

Hendrik clucked his tongue with approval and stretched his arms sideways, receiving an imaginary burst of applause.

"Look at the state he's in," Donald said. "All that stuff you've been showing him is addling his brain. Switch it off, will you?"

175

Mulder clapped his laptop shut.

Hendrik scrambled up from the floor, went over to the window and stood there, staring at the framed view of the sea as if it were a computer screen. Mulder couldn't take his eyes off him, but it was not Hendrik he saw, it was another boy, and he felt himself soaring above his own childhood, a satellite whizzing through time, until at last he collided with his stubborn youthful self silhouetted against the light. He rose from his chair and crossed to the window, wishing for the warmth of standing shoulder to shoulder, wishing he could place his hand on Hendrik's feverish neck and give him the fatherly hug Mulder himself had so desperately desired as a boy. But his arm remained by his side.

———

Donald's house was under siege from noise. The poachers were revving their buggies outside the gate and scratching the aluminium garage door with their nail-sticks. Gangsta music blared from ghetto blasters. The pounding surf damped down the din, above all at high tide and when a strong wind was blowing, but when the tide went out and the wind dropped the noise poured over the walls into the house.

Mulder sat in his room, trying to read. He could not concentrate. Not because of the tiresome youths outside the gate – their harassment would not last. There were fewer of them each day, and arriving later. Nor was he distracted by the indoor commotion: footsteps in the corridor, banging doors, barking dogs, and a lavatory forever flushing down litres of green tea and cola. Back in Paris he had learned to shut his ears to the city traffic.

His nose had a harder time of it. The house stank. Since Sarah's departure it had become infested with dirt. The cleaning woman from the under-village hadn't shown her face since the flood; she had not been injured, Winston reported, but the poachers had forbidden her to continue serving the whites on the dune. Donald neglected himself, wearing the same shirt for days. The dogs were only walked early in the morning, so they peed on the terrace. The kitchen got filthier with every improvised meal. Distressing for Mulder, who had lived alone almost all his life and who was a stickler for keeping things neat and tidy – exaggeratedly so, perhaps – but the situation was bearable because temporary.

There was something else troubling him, something that came from deep within his being. A consciousness of pain. It refused to go away. Hendrik was painful to him. It was not so much to do with the boy Mulder himself had been, more with the adult he had become: a man incapable of allowing other people into his life. He had a horror of physical proximity – dented pillows, other people's flannels, the smell of sweat, wine stains left by visitors – which had only worsened over the years. He set about cleaning up after Hendrik, laundering underwear, vacuuming the rooms, washing the kitchen floor, but his exertions merely served to rub old fears to a shine.

Mulder was angry with himself for the opportunities he had missed. He could have been a father, if only he had dared. This would be his last chance.

The plaster was removed, somewhat belatedly. Hendrik's right arm was as thin as a stalk of cinnamon, and the bone had healed at a slight angle. "We're going to build up some muscle," Donald said. At home. Hendrik was still too unpredictable for outings. Swimming in the sea was not an option for now. Donald came up with a fitness plan involving plenty of arm exercises and hopping on one leg from room to room, and back on the other leg.

But Hendrik wasn't feeling well. Not that he needed to lie down, it was his nose that was bothering him. He kept rubbing it.

"Can you smell alright?" Donald said.

No, his nose was blocked. There was some slight hindrance, something growing up his nostrils for which there wasn't enough room, what with his nose being so flat anyway. He had trouble breathing, and yet he insisted on putting a handkerchief over his nose – afraid someone would cut it off. He rubbed and rubbed. He spoke in a nasal tone, demanding a pair of sunglasses because the sun hurt his eyes. He wanted the curtains closed during the day; the half-light was soothing. He sat staring straight ahead like a zombie for hours.

As evening approached he began to hum, louder and louder. He refused to stop. The humming rose to shouting and screaming. Ignoring him didn't help, nor did persuasion. He screamed himself hoarse; his tongue was dark purple. Donald dragged him to the bathroom and put him under the shower. Coldest setting, cold turkey. Hendrik winced with pain. Mulder winced in sympathy, and wanted to leave. Donald threw him a towel. He was to scour that blerrie skin of Hendrik's till it glowed, drag the towel hard across his back and legs to get the circulation going. But Mulder could not do it.

Donald took over, rubbing the towel with unforgiving vigour and taking care to avoid the genital area. After that Mulder wound the boy into a sheet, turning him into a chaste mummy, and by the time he had finished Hendrik was yawning for bed.

———

Donald put on an apron and slid a defrosted leg of lamb into the oven. Hendrik sat slumped at the kitchen table, watching every move. Mulder sat opposite him with his book to his right, cup of

178

tea to his left, but he wasn't turning the pages and left the tea to get cold. He was reading Hendrik: the gangly posture, the anger in the hands (two fists), in the feet (shoes scraping over the tiles). Hendrik was feigning indifference, as if he couldn't care less about the luxury prison he was being held in, yet was intrigued by the light in the oven. "Do you roast meat with a lamp?" His voice sounded hoarse and nasal.

"It's an electric oven," Donald said.

Hendrik had never seen one before. And what were all those other gadgets?

Donald explained what the various electric appliances were for. He pressed oranges in the juicer, demonstrated the pop-up toaster with two slices of bread, made coffee, whipped the hot milk to a froth. Hendrik jumped up from his chair to try all the knobs. The oven lamp, however, was the most fascinating of all: "Fabulous." He knelt down in front of the oven, breathed on the glass window, wiped it clean. Donald almost tripped over him: "Mind you don't burn your fingers."

The meat sizzled. His mother roasted meat on a fire in the yard, he said. But this, this was just like television.

He yawned, from hunger this time.

———

A stone hit the terrace. Metal clanged. "The garage door," Donald sighed. He closed all the windows, drew the curtains and said they had better stay at the back of the kitchen, keep away from the glass. In case anything happened, they could get to the garage without being seen, and from there to the wine cellar. Nobody from the village knew about the cellar, not even Winston. Hendrik seemed unconcerned by the commotion. He was in Donald's study, hunched over a pile of white paper. He was drawing. On the floor beside him was a wastepaper basket overflowing with crumpled-up sheets.

"What are you drawing?" Mulder said.

"Oh, nothing."

"All those sheets of paper, all those sharpened pencils – for nothing?"

Hendrik pushed his drawing away. He had drawn a round face with a flat nose and slanting eyes. His father.

Was that what he looked like?

He shrugged. His mother had no photographs of him. But that was what he ought to look like: a Kung Fu fighter from Taiwan. YouTube was full of them. "It's him moving my pencil," Hendrik said. "He's drawing himself." But not very successfully, it seemed. Mulder glanced at the wastepaper basket. The wads of paper were moving, breathing, uncrumpling themselves. "My father's energy," Hendrik declared.

A windowpane shattered.

———

Hendrik could not be persuaded to write to his mother, he was too busy using the fountain pen to draw with. So Donald took it upon himself to write to Charmein, telling her that her son was on the mend, taking more steps in the right direction each day. Hendrik was putting on weight, his gums were healing, his eyes shone again, and the surrounding whites were less yellow. His temperature was back to normal, he was alert, his liver was no longer swollen. And he was eating greens, albeit with reluctance. They would be getting his blood checked at the hospital, and he would soon be ready to see his mother again. Donald showed Mulder the letter. "It sounds like a medical report," Mulder said. "Can't you add something a bit more personal?"

Donald complied with a postscript:

> *Hendrik has trouble getting out of bed in the morning, but even that is improving. He is supposed to be up at six, ready to come to breakfast as soon as he is called. The light in his room is switched off at ten p.m. We use the so-called shower alarm: he has to pay for each minute that he is late with two minutes under the cold shower. It is an old remedy, and still works very well. I was raised on it myself. He is making good progress, and you will soon have reason to be proud of your son again.*

The time was ripe for swimming. They went to the beach at dawn, before the under-village stirred.

Mulder and Hendrik waded into the surf together, both wearing swimming trunks borrowed from Donald. The current dragged at their waists. Hendrik shot off like a spear through the rising waves, straight and muscular, in a self-taught swimming style. Once clear of the surf he dived under the surface. Briefly, this first time.

The next day he stayed under for almost two minutes. Mulder nose-dived after him to the seabed. To his embarrassment, his arm brushed against Hendrik's, like seaweed. The sea pounded against their ears and mouths. Donald was on the shore with the dogs, waiting and watching. "You went too far out," he cried when their feet touched bottom once more. "The sea's deep and treacherous over there, and there's a cold undercurrent."

"But the gurgling sound under water's great," Hendrik said. The sea rang in his ears. He pulled up his swimming trunks: far-too-big, old-style Bermudas.

On the third morning they saw dolphins. Hendrik swam out towards them. Naked. Alone.

"Know your limits!" Donald shouted after him.

Hendrik dived and stayed under for a long time.

Mulder watched and counted. Donald stripped off his clothes, ready to go after Hendrik. The dogs trotted about restlessly. After a few scary minutes they spotted Hendrik on the crest of a wave. Raised from the deep. He swam towards the beach, grinning from ear to ear. A dolphin had given him a push, with its snout.

Donald didn't believe him.

"Oh, give him a break," Mulder said.

Hendrik was still shivering when they were back at the house having breakfast. "My blood is as cold as cola."

"So how deep did you go?" Mulder said.

"Till my eyes hurt so bad I couldn't see anymore." Some tea spilt from his shaking cup.

Donald prepared scrambled eggs and fresh orange juice.

"You know," Hendrik said with his mouth full, "your voice carries furthest where the sun doesn't shine." He had talked with the dolphins. Through closed lips. They had hummed back at him. Or it might have been a whale, a killer whale, the sort that made the water boil. Hendrik beamed, letting his imagination run wild.

Donald told him not to exaggerate. But the whale blew, the table shook, the fantasies grew. Mulder put his arm around Hendrik's shoulders – only for a second – and allowed himself to drift along on the current of lies. Hendrik ranted on.

"Calm down! Stop it!" Donald came towards them, eyes flashing with rage, unnoticed by Hendrik.

Mulder did notice, but was completely unprepared to see Donald grab hold of the fabulist's ears and give them a violent shake.

Mulder left the kitchen in a rage and made for his room. No more barking, no stamping of feet, no clamour in the road. A sudden sea mist blotted out the view from his window.

***

Hendrik shut himself up in his room – without the key, which had been confiscated as a precaution. Instead, he had pushed his bed against the door. He refused food. Donald tried to tempt him with pineapple and cola, Mulder offered him his laptop, but the only response was a dull thudding sound. He was banging his head against the wall. A relapse. Mulder and Donald were backsliding, too.

"Happy now?" Mulder said.

"Junkie behaviour," Donald said.

"What is it you want to teach him?"

"Discipline." Playing around didn't get you anywhere in South Africa. "He needs leadership. Somebody has to be the boss."

"You?"

"Hendrik and I go back a long way."

"You can see how much good that's done him."

Donald replied with a slammed door.

Mulder too holed up in his room, having no desire to rake up old grievances. Staring at the ceiling, he reflected on their friendship – or perhaps friendship was not the right word. What did they have in common? What kept them apart? Donald was serious. He believed in clear-cut solutions, structures, rules and systems, he believed in a country you could patch up like an injured patient. Mulder believed in different healing forces. After a few weeks of Fraternité, and already tired of the ideological debates, he had confessed to Donald that he couldn't abide fanatics. Fanaticism made people ugly, it affected the set of their mouths. The Chief was a case in point. People like that were one-track-minded, had a label for everything, and always had God on their side. Mulder was more of a zig-zagger, unsure as to his ultimate goal. But if there was anything he was after it was beauty, even in politics, because there was simply more beauty in a just and fair society. The gulf between rich and poor was ugly – obesity clashing with starvation. And resistance had its own aesthetic appeal. Donald had looked doubtful: "Don't let the comrades hear you."

But the comrades did hear. And he, Marten, came under fire. Pressed for an explanation, he told them about his trip to Sudan, and how the poverty there was a breeding-ground for fanatics. A foul hatred was arising, hatred of the West. Since that trip he'd read a lot about Africa, seen films and photographs, and the conclusion he'd drawn from all that information was that the only political goal left to him personally was to become the Minister of Paint. Oh, for the whole of Africa to be scaffolded and the rot, the poverty, the destitution painted over.

They had poured scorn on him. Oh, so poverty with a coat of paint meant less suffering, did it? And what colour did he have in mind? White, for sure. Donald had not come to his rescue, he sided with the comrades. The argument had escalated into a sort of kangaroo court, the outcome of which, however, was that Marten could stay, precisely because of his naïvety and ignorance about the Struggle (and his generosity: he was footing the bill). Such characteristics would work in favour of someone with a non-political mission. But he still had a lot to learn. (Quick, another round of drinks to keep them happy.) Minister of Paint . . . what a joke! Marten laughed along with them, but deep down felt defensive.

Marten's success with the group did not sit well with Donald. For the next week they managed not to cross paths, until they were summoned by old man Duriez, the Chief: the Cuban codes were waiting. *Pour la cause.* Curiosity did the rest. Marten was prepared to put up with a lot for the chance of a trip to South Africa. And so a bond was forged between them. He even grew to admire Donald for his singularity of purpose, his ambition, his commitment to his fellow man, and some of his seriousness duly rubbed off on Marten.

Mulder heard Donald shouting on the phone again. He closed his eyes and gave their friendship a fresh coat of paint.

The gate clanged shut. Winston stumbled into the unlit hallway. Donald and Mulder were in the front room, reading, and leapt up from their easy chairs. "Ring the bell first in future, will you?" Donald grumbled. "It's after ten, and Hendrik's already in bed."

Oh, the tik-head eh? Been complaining, had he? Winston roared with laughter, steadying himself against the doorpost. "That tik-head should be grateful I came over with his cola and pineapple at this hour." It was late, yes, which was a nuisance, but the suppliers had their own schedules. Surely the baas didn't think he could lug all that stuff uphill on his own in the dark of night?

"I am not your baas."

Mulder shushed their argument and helped carry the goods into the kitchen. Winston smelled of booze and the labels on the pineapple were wet: the tins had been brought in by boat.

"Smuggled?" Donald said.

Winston straightened up, scowling. Meneer was getting what he wanted, and he wasn't to think it was all plain sailing. Besides, the advance had run out, he needed more money. Prices had gone up. He wanted a drop of wine: "For my trouble."

Donald took no notice, and asked how they were getting on down in the fishing village.

Things were improving. There would soon be a proper sewage

system in place. And oh yes, another body had washed up on the beach, in a tangle of sea bamboo. The lobsters had been at it.

Mulder hid his horror by looking in the fridge for left-over wine. He thought of Riempie, and of the shell diver in the surf.

Winston was handed a small glass of wine. He sat himself down and turned up the left sleeve of his overalls to show off his new, shiny Rolex. Bought from a Chinese vendor in the parking lot.

Mulder tapped admiringly on the extra-thick glass face of the watch while Donald checked the contents of his wallet, frowning. It was high time he called at his bank in Distriksdorp, seeing as they were both out of cash. "We can't leave Hendrik on his own yet. You'll have to wait for your money."

Winston shambled over to the sink, patted the toaster, picked up an antique cutlery box and rattled it.

"What are you looking for, Winston?" Donald said.

"Cape silver?"

"Put that back, Winston."

"Yes, Faan." Winston picked at his nails. His fingers gave off a smell of fresh resin.

From the beach where they went swimming to Donald's house it was at least two miles of soft sand and a steep climb. Hendrik covered the distance without apparent exertion, revelling in having beaten his own record – a few more seconds under water each day. Getting his strength back meant a growing desire for independence, and he found it increasingly irksome to walk with Donald and Mulder on either side of him. He longed to charge up the dunes on his own, and at the first whiff of a cooking fire to race down to his old home at the bottom of the fishing village. The water had receded, there was a possibility that some of his mother's stuff was still lying around. "What do you hope to find there?" Donald said, adding that her bed had no doubt been used for firewood.

Hendrik was thinking of the china cat from Taiwan.

"Later," Donald said. "Not now."

Hendrik pleaded with them after each swimming session, but the answer was always no. Until one day he broke away just as they were reaching the gate, and ran off towards the harbour, pursued for some distance by Mulder. Donald sent the dogs after him, "Go on! get him," but the Artois merely bounded along at Hendrik's heels, and returned without him.

Donald went to the garage to get the car out, but the lock was yet again clogged up with resin. It was still runny. He ran into the house to try to raise the swing door from the inside. Mulder waited in the road. He could hear Donald cursing and banging on the door. It wouldn't budge. "I'll have to smash it," Donald said, and began to batter the tough aluminium with the sharp end of an axe. The noise was deafening, the metal bulged out and buckled, but the door still wouldn't budge. "Keep clear! I'm going to shoot out the lock."

Mulder ducked away: "Steady now, easy." One shot, two . . . Donald emptied the chamber firing at the door. Smoke curled round the edges. The dogs yelped and bit their tails in fright.

More blows with the axe, aimed at the circle of bullet holes. The lock tumbled out, the garage door began to rise, but soon the warped frame got jammed in the guide rails. They pushed the door up as far as it would go. Donald started the 4x4. "You stay here," he called, swearing as he pulled away at speed.

Mulder found a broom and swept up the debris. The dogs cowered in their basket. Gulls screeched overhead and voices could be heard in the distance. An alarm went off.

A ridgeback appeared, wagging its tail. And another, closely followed by the neighbour with the pistol. He was panting from the effort. "What's up? You guys still alive?"

"False alarm," Mulder said, trying to sound casual.

"And those shots?" The neighbour inspected the bullet holes in the door. "Al Capone been here, has he?" He picked up a spent cartridge and assessed it with narrowed eyes. "Serious stuff, this. Top quality . . . Ah well, taking a tik-head under your wing is sort of asking for it, really. The police are no match for those gangs."

"The problem has been dealt with. He's gone, anyway."

"The French food didn't agree with him, then?" The neighbour spluttered with laughter. "It's no good uprooting a pumpkin. That boy grew up in a shack, they still cook on paraffin there."

Mulder gave a shrug. "You've been to his house, I take it?"

"What's that supposed to mean?" He never went down the hill himself. But he'd heard stories. Donald received visits from prostitutes! Yes, in the end it was all his own fault: big-headed Donald stirring up trouble among the fishing folk, setting them against their own leaders. The neighbour pulled up his shorts and draped his belly over his belt. "It's thanks to your lot that it's so unsafe around here nowadays."

Mulder patted a ridgeback, muttering, "I'm only passing through, you know." A gutless excuse.

Stienie came running, shaking with nerves. She too had heard the shots. The police had already been called. Had the skollies been at it again? Kobus and she had taken a stroll before bed last night, and they'd seen somebody in the shadows by the gate, fiddling with the lock. And there were baddies lurking there in the daytime, too. It was the house, she said, there was a curse on the house. It didn't belong somehow, not in the white area, not in the dunes, it was too isolated and forbidding, with its back up against the rest.

Forbidding or not, there was now a breach in the enclosure: a gaping garage giving access to a terrace. The neighbour with the pistol said it was too dangerous to leave the swing door open, so the three men joined forces to drag it down They kicked the twisted metal into place as best they could. The neighbour was out of breath. "I smoke too much, but then cancer gives a sense of certainty in uncertain times." He laughed to camouflage his cough.

A blue butterfly flitted around Stienie's flushed head. Mulder was seized with an intense longing for a cold winter in Paris.

Half an hour later the 4x4 drove up to the house, with a wan-looking Hendrik huddled on the back seat. Donald had found him at the bottom of the village, just where he expected: by the remains of Charmein's drowned house. He'd been obliged to leave his car and walk the last bit because the road was too narrow, and his clothes were streaked with dirt. Hendrik said nothing, and kept his jaws clenched as he was led inside to the sofa in the sitting room. He left his glass of cola untouched and pushed the pineapple offering away. Just sat there, making no sound or movement.

Mulder and Donald closed the terrace doors and barricaded the garage. No more need of Winston. They worked themselves into a sweat. Donald took off his shirt – there was an angry red swelling on his back. A stone thrown by a poacher. He didn't want to talk about it. "It's O.K. Just as long as Hendrik makes it."

Donald rang the hospital in Distriksdorp, and was eventually able to talk to Charmein. She could now walk a little, but had to undergo a second operation.

"Would you like to speak to Hendrik?" Donald said. She wasn't eager, but he insisted. "He misses you."

190

Hendrik shook his head vehemently. Donald thrust the receiver into his hand

"Hello?"

"Hello."

Minutes of silence ensued. Then the line went dead.

Relapse, his second. Hendrik had a high fever, he shivered, his sheets were drenched with sweat. His blood pressure soared, his pulse raced, his urine was dark yellow and he shouted and screamed in his dreams, all night long. Donald checked his medicine cabinet: sleeping tablets were in order. The following evening he and Mulder took them, too, and slept like logs. That was the night the car was set on fire. A bottle of petrol had been hurled at it.

Five minutes later Winston was back in the hallway, clattering about to rouse Donald. All the neighbours had come running, some of them were already putting out the flames. Donald stood there yawning. He didn't care, he said, he couldn't care less. And Winston was to get the hell out of there. Plenty of tinned food in the house anyway, although the freezer was almost empty.

Hendrik persisted in his muteness. Days of silence went by.

A full moon, 3 a.m., and a wakeful Mulder lay in bed listening to the sounds of the night. Familiar sounds, but also a new one: the muffled beat of reggae music. He got up and saw a slit of blue light under the kitchen door. Hendrik was hunched over the laptop, tap-tap. He did not look up, did not did acknowledge Mulder's presence, his eyes were glued to the screen. Mulder made tea and looked over Hendrik's shoulder: Bob Marley crooning a lazy song

"Rasta," Hendrik said. "I want to be a Rasta." His first utterance after days of stubborn silence.

The following day he refused to wash his hair. Two swimming sessions later it was matted and stiff with salt. Reggae music percollated through the rooms. Dozens of videos came past, concerts in smoke-filled venues. Then he discovered punk – now that was something! The windowpanes rattled. Hendrik made himself a necklace of linked safety pins, and cut the sleeves off an old black T-shirt Donald had given him. And those shiny rubber boots in the guest room, might he borrow them? Mulder was taken aback: "Have you been nosing around in my suitcase?" Five minutes later they had a swaggering punk on their hands.

Then Hendrik decided being a Chinese punk would be even better, with hair sticking up all over and a spider's web tattoo on his elbow. Getting the hair to form upright spikes was not a success, but he spent hours drawing the web on his elbow with a felt tip pen. The ink wore off in the sea.

The day after that he wanted to be a "jazzing and jiving Boesman." The Boesman singers had almond eyes, too, like his. No, not Zulu or Xhosa, that wouldn't work, although Zulu music was cool.

"You can be all of them," Donald said.

But Hendrik would have none of it. "I'm not a mix, because if you are you're nothing, like brackish water – not fresh, not salt either." Being coloured was an invention of the whites, to make him invisible – no past, no tribe, no clan, no loyalty. The Zulus had their Shaka, the Afrikaners had their Jan van Riebeeck, but what did the coloureds have? They didn't even have a language of their own.

"Where did you get all those ideas from?"

Internet. Hendrik's head was full of the internet.

After the beach one day Donald and Mulder took him to the shell midden, the sacred ground of the fishers. "This is where your mother's ancestors used to come together. There's Khoikhoi blood in you, too. You're a son of the oldest people of southern Africa."

Hendrik poked around in the clotted shells. "Beach walkers," he scoffed. "Hotnots."

"You should be proud." Donald traced the routes taken by whites and Khoikhoi, with yet more enthusiasm than he had displayed earlier to Mulder. "They were herdsmen, cattle-breeders, free people. Their language has influenced yours and mine too."

After an afternoon of browsing the internet Hendrik was able to beat Donald at his own game. The Khoi had been slaves like the rest. What did he mean by saying they were free? The men had been massacred and the women raped. Three clicks on the laptop and a history of endless intermingling unfolded on the screen, with black Africa, Asia and Europe trickling down to the Cape. The Khoikhoi dissolved into all three.

Hendrik was proud of his discovery. It was as easy as pie, he said, you just typed "hotnot" in the search bar. "Me, I don't have slave blood in my veins, and even if I do have a drop, I'll piss it out like I pissed out the tik." He closed the laptop.

Donald patted him on the shoulder. "You're even smarter than I thought."

Mulder smiled contentedly as he gave his laptop a quick polish with his handkerchief. At the evening meal they linked hands, not to say a prayer; they just hoped aloud that Hendrik would be alright, and shed a tear as they did so.

Plop. The dogs had found a sachet of white powder on the terrace, which, with much tail-wagging, was dropped at Donald's feet. A gift from the poachers? Donald took it to the kitchen, shook a little of the contents on a saucer, dipped his finger in it and tasted warily.

Tik? Hendrik would be able to tell – just by looking, mind you! He recognised the sachet. Yes, it was tik.

Donald wanted to fire a few shots in the air to scare off the skollies hanging around the gate, but Mulder managed to dissuade him. "They're better armed than we are." He took a pinch of the powder and placed it on the palm of his hand, glancing around in triumph, but before he could take a sniff Donald gave him a slap on the wrist. Mulder sneezed, and blew half the powder across the table. "Don't be ridiculous," Donald burst out. "Have you no sense of responsibility at all?" Hendrik ran to the tap to rinse off the saucer. Snorting it was too much, he said, you were supposed to boil the stuff and inhale the fumes. No, not on a spoon, you used a light bulb – knock off the fitting, put the powder in, hold a flame underneath until it bubbles, inhale, and wait until your brains crash against your skull. He reeled it off without emotion.

Donald emptied the sachet in the sink. Mulder ran his finger over the remaining traces on the table and licked it furtively. His tongue tingled and he felt the blood rising to his head.

By the time paradise broke loose he was in the bathroom, splashing his face with cold water. The tiles began to dance, and he had to hold on to the basin to steady himself for the onslaught of giddy euphoria. His heart fluttered like a hummingbird, his ribcage ceased to be a cage. He saw himself in the mirror: stronger now, untroubled. He rose up above his body. He was weightless, flying. Just for a moment, then his parched tongue dragged him back into his solid self. He found himself staring at a wall of white tiles, with a vile taste in his mouth.

Music blared in the kitchen. Hendrik spent all afternoon engrossed in YouTube. China was top favourite again, with Brain Failure as the premiere band. Post-punk, groovy songs, heavy stuff. Unintelligible, too, but for a few phrases in English. Mulder couldn't stand the noise, but Hendrik clapped hard after each track. *"Living in the city, there's no fashion. Living in the city, turn on the electric. Anarchy, anarchy."* Four times in succession.

Donald was in his study talking to Sarah on the phone. He too was shouting. Her car had been parked at the airport for weeks, and he wanted the spare keys: *"Les clés! Où sont tes putains de clés?"* Mulder had a headache and wanted to take a nap, but the guestroom was too noisy, so he went down the long corridor in search of a quieter spot – at least half the rooms were not in use. The far end of the corridor was Sarah's domain. The door to her work room was ajar. Donald avoided that part of the house. He didn't even want it vacuumed, saying everything had to remain exactly as Sarah had left it, the dustier the better. Normally, the door was locked. Now that it wasn't, Mulder couldn't resist taking a peek inside. It was a large room, double doors to an east-facing terrace, walls faced with lavender-blue linen, fluffy white rugs on the floor. By far the most French-looking room in the house, with an antique secretaire and an Art Deco dressing table. The double bed suggested that

195

it must have been the master bedroom at one time. Mulder had already gathered that Sarah and Donald had stopped sleeping together years ago. Donald's preferred bed was a divan in his study.

Mulder wanted to turn back, but the intruder in him was already standing by the dressing table laden with brushes, combs, hairdryer, jars and tubes of cosmetics. He sniffed at a bottle of Hermès *Eau des Merveilles*. His eyes were drawn to the secretaire in the far corner: a further intimation of privacy. The lid was raised, the drawers were open and ransacked. Various keys lay on the blotter, along with insurance papers and a driving licence. On the upper ledge stood a framed family photograph showing a father wearing a straw boater, chin raised, and a plumpish mother flanked by a son in some kind of uniform, and a timid-looking younger daughter with a slightly flattened nose. Mulder studied the family of four posing in front of a large white villa on a dune. He recognised the wide roof and the oval garden gate, only the walls seemed less high and the garden less lush. It was Donald's house. And the boy in the uniform was young Faan Treghardt – who else?

On an impulse, Mulder took the photograph out of its frame and slid it under his shirt. He was excited about his discovery – but regretted his action on the instant. The photograph was curling at the corners, and he didn't dare put it back where it belonged as he could hear the dogs trotting down the corridor. They entered, wagging their tails and giving little yaps of recognition as they caught the scent of their mistress. Fearing exposure, Mulder opened the doors to the terrace and shooed the dogs outside, only to find Hendrik hovering nearby. Mulder muttered something about the dogs being a nuisance. Hendrik leaned into the room, past the billowing curtains, and touched the lavender wall. He had never seen such a beautiful room. Mulder made to close the terrace doors, but Hendrik had already slipped inside, pointing to the chrome hairdryer on the dressing table. "What's that? A gun?"

"An electric hairdryer."

Hendrik wanted to try it out, but Mulder hustled him out into the corridor.

"Why do whites have everything electric?"

"Well, think of that Chinese song," Mulder said, turning to go back to his room. "Living in the city, turn on the electric." Gosh, he actually remembered the words.

After supper Donald and Mulder opened a bottle of white wine on the front terrace, under the parasol, where the balmy air of the day still lingered. They had abstained for more than a week, for the sake of setting a good example, but now they had something to celebrate: Hendrik was making progress. That being the case, they were less inclined to fight over him. "We both do what we can," Donald sighed.

"Were we like that when we were young?" Mulder wondered. "Imagine if they'd been handing out that shit in the schoolyard in our day."

"Well, when I was a kid they'd sniff my clothes every day in case I'd been smoking. Hendrik's trouble is that he's lacked rules and supervision."

"And you liked rules?"

Donald heaved a sigh. "I was supposed to be a good example."

Mulder said that he had been pretty scared as a teenager, but that his curiosity had always got the better of him, which was why he had come into contact with everything God had forbidden early on.

They called up memories of their shared "dangerous moments" in Paris, with those amphetamines to keep you going all night, and weird little pills to get you dancing like crazy. Hash was for the slow movers. Revolutionaries were more into booze. And sex? Yes well, you lasted a bit longer with a dab of coke on your dick – or scouring powder, because you had no way of telling if you'd been ripped off. And crab lice, yes, there were those as well. All those hassles being passed around, but perhaps that was part of the thrill . . . They dropped the subject, all unpleasantness was to be avoided.

But the photograph kept nagging at the back of Mulder's mind. The family portrait with goody-goody Donald in his uniform. Donald had actually lived here, in this house, as a boy. He had inherited it from his old man! Then why hadn't he said so, why the false shame? Mulder was eager to ask, but didn't want to spoil the atmosphere. He would wait for the right moment. The photograph was in his room, underneath the Bible. He had intended to put it back, but Sarah's door was locked again.

They were startled by a high-pitched buzz coming from the house. Was Hendrik busy with the laptop? He was not at the kitchen table. Where had he got to?

They called to him, then followed the buzzing sound down the corridor to his room. They knocked. No reply. The door wouldn't open – blocked by the bed, no doubt. Donald gave the door a hard kick. The buzzing stopped. They heard the scrape of furniture, and after a long moment Hendrik opened the door. His hair stood up on end, and he was wearing black eyeliner. Sarah's hairdryer lay on the bed.

Donald exploded. "How did you get hold of that? I don't want you touching Sarah's things. You look like a whore."

198

Hendrik ducked away, but Donald grabbed him by his blow-dried hair. "Get in the shower, you! Now!"

The boy howled in protest, but Donald held him tight and frog-marched him the length of the corridor. Mulder held back, for fear of being the accomplice to the next round of torture, and having to flog Hendrik dry with the towel. He felt paralysed by Donald's rage. He heard the shower gushing, the cries – felt the jets of cold water, the manhandling, the pain. In his mind he lashed out at Donald, but in reality slunk off to his room for the photograph and returned with it to the terrace.

The commotion in the bathroom was followed by doors being slammed, and a moment later Donald burst onto the terrace, dripping wet. "Why did you let me down like that?"

Mulder gave him a withering look. "So you don't think Hendrik is man enough, is that it?" He held up the photograph.

Donald snatched it from him. "Where did you get this from?"

"I thought we agreed we would do everything in Hendrik's best interests. You're undoing all the good we've just done."

"Have you been snooping around as well? You know that's something I'm allergic to."

"Creepy outfit you're wearing there."

Donald dropped into a chair and studied the photograph. "Oh, that uniform doesn't mean anything. It was like being a Boy Scout, only we were called Voortrekkers. Yes, we all wore that."

"You've inherited your father's chin." Mulder refilled their glasses. Hendrik was slouching across the far end of the terrace on his way to the laptop in the kitchen. He looked tearful.

"I wonder if I've been too harsh on him," Donald mused. Then, addressing the boy in the photograph: "Just look at you, standing to attention, full of respect. No indeed, my pa was never contradicted.

Not at home. Not in our neighbourhood either. All my friends were in awe of him. Most of the grown-ups too, as a matter of fact."

"Did the people round here know what he stood for, do you think?" Mulder said.

"He was known all over the country back then. His picture was in the papers, he was always giving speeches in public."

"And the fishers, did they know?"

"No idea, until recently they didn't read newspapers. But the whites were all treated with respect, genuine or not. The old folk still call me baas. You've no idea how hard it's been to get people to call me Donald."

"But I suppose that name took some getting used to, anyway," Mulder said, as innocently as he could.

"Well, they soon switched to calling me 'Doctor'."

"Tell me about your sister."

"It's one of the very few pictures with her in it, as it happens." Donald took a sip of tepid wine and pushed his glass away, wrinkling his nose. "My sister was dark-skinned, she looked coloured. There was some mixed ancestry in my ma's family, which my ma was at pains to keep secret when she married, but then the colour of her daughter's skin gave her away. My pa destroyed all her family albums after my sister was born. She was his Achilles heel. He was sleeping with the enemy, so to speak. He, the pure-blooded Afrikaner whose children had to be kept out of the sun."

"Scared. Typical racist."

"But a racist who loved Africa, in his own way. At home he enthused about the brilliant black students he had met during his tours of duty, but at the Ministry, behind his desk, he ripped their families apart at the stroke of a pen, banishing mothers and children to the remotest homelands. I know that he paid for a couple

200

of boys to go to university – a black university, needless to say. On a personal level he may well have done more good than all those high-minded folks we hung around with in Paris." He laid the photograph on the table. "Not that I'm absolving him of all blame, mind you."

"So now it's your turn to do good in a coloured village."

"I've grown attached to this place, yes."

"You've been attached to it for ages, it seems to me." Mulder forced himself not to quiz Donald further.

Donald rubbed his goose-pimpled arms. The laptop was blaring in Hendrik's room: Chinese punks screaming for electricity. "Should I go and apologise to him?"

"Later," Mulder said. "Give him a chance to wallow in his hatred for a bit."

They uncorked another bottle from the fridge despite their good intentions – more wine to quench burning issues.

"By the way," Mulder ventured after several minutes of silence, "why didn't you go back after graduating from medical school? You could've been healing the sick over here. More useful than playing the revolutionary in Paris, surely."

Donald sighed. "Politics, politics . . . Anyway, my hands shook. I soon switched to the theoretical side. Research was not a calling in my case, it was my fate." He took a gulp of wine. "If I hadn't left I'd have been swallowed up by the system straight away. Before you know it, you're one of them."

"Is that why you went to Paris? Is that why you got involved in the resistance – to free yourself from your background?"

"That, too," Donald murmured, looking away.

"But it wasn't a holiday, it was hardship. You broke with your family and with your language. You were homesick as hell. An exile like the rest of the comrades, you were just as poor, and you felt just as African as they did. There was one thing that made you stand out, though: your principles, which were higher than anybody else's." Mulder's sarcasm was lost on Donald. "You paid your own way as a student cleaning hospitals, you missed your mother's funeral, you lost contact with your father for good."

"I wasn't allowed into the country," Donald said coldly. "You know that."

"The price of resistance. Poor you, inheriting only an old topographic map, out of date and useless." Mulder stood up, closed the parasol and switched the outside light on – the glaring burglar light. Bats flitted away. "Stop the pretence, Donald. The whole village knows it's your father's house you're living in."

Donald turned away. "Turn that damn light off."

Mulder leaned over to him: "You played here as a kid, hung around on this very terrace – small-baas Faan, son of the fearsome Treghardt. No wonder you spotted that snake's trail in the nature reserve, no wonder you recognised the porcupine tracks! We're right in the middle of your childhood here. Don't talk to me about Hotnots blood – you were a keen Boy Scout, that's what!"

"Has Winston said anything?"

"The whole village is gossiping, but this photograph says it all, doesn't it?"

"We used to come here for the holidays. The summer house was left to me."

Donald's hand shook as he poured more wine. "My father and I were reconciled shortly before he died. I'm sorry, I should have told you before." He made to stand up, but Mulder put his hand on Donald's arm.

"No point in feeling guilty, for God's sake. You might as well enjoy what you've got."

"My pa came over to Paris to see me after my mother died. He begged me to return. South Africa needed me, he needed me. He used every means of persuasion: God, our language, his capital. Catherine was already in jail by then. I blamed him for that, but he said it wasn't his fault, that he hadn't had anything to do with her arrest. For a time he thought he had enough clout to secure her release, but he was up against greater monsters, monsters of his own making." Donald watched the flight of a pair of bats. "He fell on his knees and asked me to forgive him."

"And you gave in, sort of. It doesn't matter, you weren't the only one. But why make such a big thing of it? You were the most serious of us all back in Paris, always on the lookout for betrayal, because you didn't trust yourself either. You didn't want to be like your father, but he's right there deep inside you. You wanted to break with the Afrikaner clan, but that's part of you as well. And so is bloody apartheid, just as it is for the rest of your generation. A conse-quence of growing up in a sick society. But you always claimed to have the purest of motives. It was all a question of rational analysis, not sentiment. Really? You're as much of a wimp as I am. You fell for the same woman as I did. What you kept from me was that you already knew Catherine before you left South Africa, that her parents and yours knew each other. I saw your father with her at Die Hugenoot, and yet you have the gall to suggest that I betrayed her." Mulder hit the table with the flat of his hand.

Donald shrank back in his chair. "I didn't think my father ever visited them . . . and it was my handwriting on the envelope. Still, I thought I was being clever. Conservative families were above suspi-cion at the time."

"So that makes us even," Mulder said. "Because it was my fault that the envelope was still lying there."

"Yeah, for a long time I believed, or wanted to believe, that it was you who betrayed her. Out of base fear. Just you, then at least I'd know it wasn't anybody else."

"So that's why you invited me over." Mulder shook his head sadly.

"Catherine was reckless."

"And so were you, so was I. They were reckless times. Betrayal is made up of a thousand minor slip-ups, careless mistakes like the presence of an onion in your luggage, traces of cordite on your collar, too many pencil dots in a Bible, ill-advised love affairs, wrong accents. You take risks, seek adventure, think you're invincible, and the traitor is always somebody else: the comrade working under-cover for the security police, the Chief toying with his pawns."

Donald spluttered in protest.

"And now we ourselves are the traitors. By chance. We just don't know."

They held each other's eyes for a long moment, trying to detect the monster within. But they did not succeed, for the least inkling of such a presence was efficiently drowned in more wine.

They drank all night. Genies were let out of bottles, filling the air with fathers, and with politics too – the nefarious power of poli-tics. They crept down to the wine cellar. Donald opened forbidden vintages, they wrinkled their noses at corked wines, took a magnum upstairs. And they turned up the music, setting off the dogs. Winston appeared on the terrace, jangling his big bunch of keys. He said somebody had offered to buy the wrecked 4x4. "That's it," Donald fumed, "I'm getting a proper locksmith to come over tomorrow, and you'll never set foot in here again."

Old scratchy records of Masekela and Dollar Brand were played. They went out to the terrace and did a theatrical dance together, exchanging insults, profuse apologies, warm embraces. They were roaring drunk, but they knew what they were doing. They broke apart, then staggered into each other's arms again, and were suddenly aware of being watched. Hendrik was standing at the window.

It was afternoon by the time Donald and Mulder woke up, in spite of the dogs. The terrace stank of urine, the house was quiet. No tapping on the laptop, no punk bands. Only billowing curtains and an occasional door banging in the wind. Hendrik was nowhere to be seen. His bed was rumpled, but not slept in; his bath towel was dry. The kitchen table was strewn with torn-up drawings of his imagined father, the Kung Fu fighter from Taiwan. A token of goodbye.

Mulder's laptop was missing, his small rucksack, his suitcase, and the laces were gone from his shoes. The borrowed rubber boots were gone too. Donald charged about the house, cursing. One of the shelves in his wardrobe was bare: not a single T-shirt left. And Sarah's door had been forced. The hairdryer no longer lay on the dressing table. They lamented all their losses, as though each item were a part of Hendrik.

How could they have been so stupid? So drunk, so careless, so trusting. They didn't dare count the empty bottles. Should they ring the police? Or should they go out in search of him themselves, and confess their debacle to Charmein?

They laid the table for three. Fried eggs for three. The quiet spoiled their appetite. Mulder switched on the radio, twiddled the dial until he found some music. "Will he go back to the tik, d'you think?" he asked as he crushed two aspirins to a powder.

"The poachers will have been waiting for him," Donald said. "They won't let him go until he's had another hit."

"But surely, now that he's got to know a different world . . ."

"Indeed. And a fine example we've been setting, haven't we?"

Not until they cleared the breakfast things away did they notice that the Cape silver cutlery box was missing. And that the gate was ajar. There was resin on the inside of the lock, too. No way of closing the gate.

A couple of hours later the locksmith arrived from Distriksdorp. All the locks were replaced, and arrangements made for a new garage door to be installed, as well as electrified fencing on three sides, four lines high. The Armed Response service was called – burly, bull-necked individuals providing security systems for the rich. Donald had never wanted anything to do with them, but now he found himself with his back against his own wall.

There was music in the harbour. New boats lay on the slipway, from which the mud had been cleared, and the flag was hoisted on the pier. Coils of smoke rose from the refurbished fried-squid stall behind the cold store. Children nibbled doughnuts. Booths had been set up in the parking lot, where free condoms were distributed and free Party wine was poured from cardboard boxes into plastic cups. Fishers, poachers, old crones, grandpas and young mothers, all were merry. The under-village was celebrating the instalment of the first hundred metres of sewer pipes. The mayor had donated a hundred metres of dried sausage. Mulder trod on a carpet of discarded sausage-skins. He was making a final round of the view from his former window. A taxi would take him to Cape Town the following morning. He said goodbye to the girls lounging against cars and to a couple of oyster-sellers, but did not shake any hands. He inhaled the mingled aromas of salt-encrusted skirts, tepid shells and sea bamboo.

At the foot of his dune entire families lay sprawled, sleeping off the wine. Only the infants were open-eyed. Mulder walked close to the tide-line, skipping clear of the unfurling foam, thick with plankton, and getting his shoes wet anyway. He didn't mind – salt marks on leather would make a nice souvenir. Nobody paid any attention to him, except for a child offering him a piece of sausage.

The sun went down, tingeing the sand with crimson before the swift descent of night. Striking up the narrow track into the dunes, he bumped into Karneels, unshaven and unsteady on his feet, hugging a box of wine. "All alone are you? Poor Meneer!"

He would not let Mulder pass unless he promised to share a drink. The mayor was not the only one being generous – so was Karneels, his habitual deference now dissolved in wine. They went to sit on a rise in the dune and took turns to slurp the wine from the tap on the box.

"What do the Doctor and Meneer want with that boy?"

"To give him a future."

"A future for one fish, leaving all the others gasping in the mud."

"Better to save one than to let them all stew."

"Save? There's been talk . . ." Karneels gave the box a shake to check how much wine was left. "The Doctor goes in the shower with him, no clothes on. You and the Doctor dance together. Two men dancing."

"And what of it?"

"Charges have been brought."

Just one suitcase in the taxi – not Mulder's. His was floating around elsewhere, and he now had to travel as he had always wanted to, and that was light. He had even left his beloved wooden shoe trees behind in the guestroom. The suitcase belonged to Donald, whose lawyer had strongly advised him to go into hiding after the latest piece of gossip. Mulder too had urged him to make himself scarce for a bit.

The charge was being processed and everybody was talking about it. There was little point in trying to defend yourself against false rumours, and besides, the chief witness was missing. Or was Hendrik the one pressing charges? Mulder had rung the door-bells of all the neighbours, but nobody had seen a teenager with a red suitcase in the early hours of the morning, and none of them emerged from behind their intercoms except Stienie, who asked him to step inside, as her husband was out fishing anyway. She had heard the news. Donald wasn't someone she considered a friend, really, but she had been willing to ring her maid, who knew everybody in the under-village and whose son was a poacher. No sign of Hendrik in those circles either.

What about Winston, then, where was he? That evening Mulder had gone to the hotel and found Karneels in the bar. Had he heard anything? Well, Karneels' grandpa had gone off to town.

The bar had been full of regulars nursing their drinks as usual while the latest cricket jokes were exchanged. They had given Mulder meaningful looks. Someone behind him had muttered: "Why doesn't he go and drink with the fishers?"

An hour before the taxi was due Mulder called the hospital, as Donald couldn't face speaking to Charmein. She was furious. Hendrik could go to hell, Donald could go to hell, and yes, so could Mulder for all she cared. In the old days they'd have put Hendrik in prison, and he'd have kicked the habit by now.

Donald sighed. He steeled himself to phone the Major. A lengthy conversation ensued, the gist of which was simple: Hendrik was a lost cause.

It was to be Donald's first taxi ride in his own country. Hunched on the low back seat with his knees drawn up high, he looked round at his imposing villa as the car pulled away. The newly fortified garage door gleamed in the sun. A scattering of beer cans testified to the siege by the poachers, not one of whom had shown his face since Hendrik's disappearance. Noting the blackened, blistered 4x4, the taxi driver asked, "Accident?"

"No, bad boys," Donald said.

Ah. Hard luck. Was Meneer thinking of selling the wreck, by any chance?

"You can have it," Donald said. "Just as long as you keep your trap shut for the rest of the journey." Mulder poked him with his elbow, but Donald was too enraged for polite conversation. As far as he was concerned they could burn the whole place down, then he could go and live in Paris as well, from the insurance money.

"With Sarah?" Mulder said.

Donald glared out of the window, his slender fingers trembling on his knee. The driver turned the air conditioning up full blast. He was following their conversation in the rear-view mirror.

Mulder tried to placate Donald: "You could sell up, start a new life."

"A new life? This place is my life, this landscape." His saliva sprayed on the window. "I'd only miss it, I'd only wither away in Paris, just like in the old days. You have no idea how happy I was here as a child. Back home in Pretoria there was always a policeman in a car stationed outside the door, and unfamiliar voices in the hallway keeping me awake at night. Here on the coast I never felt scared. One day I climbed up to the top of the highest dune all by myself, with a view stretching all the way to Antarctica. Once, after a storm, I spotted icebergs through my binoculars... Just imagine, icebergs off the coast of Africa!" The triumph of a Voortrekker Boer. Being able to tell Mulder these things at last was a relief to him.

They drove round a wide bend, and as Donald turned to look back at the dunes Mulder could see the yearning in his shoulders. "Why can't you just live on the coast in an ordinary way? No guilt, no moral obligations, no expectations."

"Ordinary?" Donald tugged pensively at his lapels. "Is there such a thing as ordinary love? You love another person for the traits you yourself lack. The sea has washed my ambitions away, I'd like to live a simpler life, be content with less, go with the ebb and the flow, like the fishers. Be more African. It's hard to explain in words, but the main reason I came back was to learn."

Mulder had to bite his tongue not to make snide remarks. Only rich people wanted to be happy with less. And what sort of idea did Donald have about Africa, anyway? A continent sitting on its arse being simple? Hadn't he seen all that bling-bling round the poachers' necks? Softening, Mulder came up with: "To learn? But you were always putting your oar in."

"I wanted to do something in return."

The duneland receded in the rear window as they passed the ostrich farm, with the mannetjies racing alongside the car as usual. The baboons with their young were waiting at the roadside again, begging for titbits. Mulder leaned out and threw them a few biscuits – the last ones from the larder.

"Don't feed the baboons," Donald grumbled.

The veld stretched out into the distance, scores of bokkies shot away through the tall grass. Mulder sat on the edge of his seat in the back, craning to look. This was something he would remember for the rest of his life, he said. "Just look at them with their fluttery little ears, their long leaping legs, their flying haunches – what a wonderful sight, what a privilege to be here!"

"That's why we're so deeply attached to this country," Donald said. He fell silent, staring out of the window. As they reached the hills, long after they had left the bokkies behind, he blurted, "Deep down I have this fear of not belonging here."

The tarmac simmered, the breeze was scented with herbs. The driver pursed his lips and kept an eye on his rear-view mirror.

The cash dispenser rattled obediently, the taxi driver was handed the keys of the burnt-out 4x4, and the passengers were dropped off at the Mount Nelson Hotel, five stars at the foot of Table Mountain. At Mulder's insistence.

"But we aren't dressed for it," Donald protested.

"No problem, at this sort of place the clientele tend to have more money than taste."

Donald cringed visibly in the spacious lobby, overcome by the colonial splendour. He stared at his sandy shoes. A bellboy took charge of his suitcase and the doorman offered to have his jacket pressed. Mulder slipped a banknote to each man. Donald blinked several times.

"Tips are a good starter," Mulder said under his breath. "Retrospective generosity doesn't pay." He was glad to be taking the lead for a change, and besides, he was on familiar ground: creaky parquet floors, thick Persian rugs, portraits in oils, grand stairways and long, corset-pink corridors. He liked a bit of grandeur.

"Hasn't changed much," he said on the way to the bar. "Do you realise it was thanks to you that I first set foot in this place?"

Donald did not remember. It had been an assignment in the Cuban code: Marten was supposed to do a recce of the hotel, find out whether the newspaper kiosk might serve as a drop-off point. He had taken the opportunity to have a drink in the bar – holding his glass of port in his left hand in honour of Horatio Nelson, who lost his right arm in the battle of Tenerife. Mulder gave a slight bow in the direction of the admiral's portrait. Wouldn't this be an appropriate place to dine this evening?

Donald was unenthusiastic. Was there not somewhere less stuffy? He tilted his head towards the signed photograph of Churchill on the wall. "This is redneck territory. They're still celebrating the Boer War here," he growled (in imitation of the bulldog behind glass). No, the Nelson was no good. What use could it have been as a drop-off point anyway? "No black comrade would have made it past the servants' quarters."

"You'd be surprised," Mulder said. "There was plenty of plotting and scheming going on in the background. The restaurant was exempt from the colour bar, anyway. You had people of all colours dining there – which was inconceivable in any of the other top hotels in the Cape. They pissed in the same stalls. Small-scale apartheid didn't exist here."

"Not for foreigners, perhaps."

"Nor for the South African elite, what with a drink costing as much as a black made in a week – and a meal the equivalent of a white weekly wage."

"And you consorted with that lot?" Donald exclaimed in disbelief.

They ordered port wine and clinked glasses, left-handedly.

"From the balcony here you had a view of the old harbour, and you could watch the supply vessel for Robben Island putting out to sea."

"Just shows how far you stuck your neck out."

Mulder gave a guilty chuckle. Even back then, forty years ago, he'd had qualms about enjoying that view.

———

They had been play-acting, although she was fearful about her role (the Law! the Law!). But they had adopted an elaborate disguise, she in a knee-length Stuttafords dress (a gift, exchangeable at the store) and Marten in a blazer with a gold-embroidered oak leaf on the breast pocket. She was being an American tourist with straightened hair; he a Hollander, dumb but loaded.

She spoke with an exaggerated American accent. He kept his voice down. It was a game . . . they found each other in dissemblance. They drank port, holding their glasses in their left hands, and he leaned over to kiss her on the cheek. She smelled of cheap make-up, and vaguely of petrol from the covered car park. They attracted notice. Drinking across the colour bar was permitted. But kissing across the colour bar?

The second time the barman came to their table to wipe it down, he asked her about America. Where was she from: East Coast, West Coast?

West Coast, she said.

L.A.?

She was at a loss. "Los Angeles," Marten whispered – too late. Their cover was blown. The barman ordered them to leave. Outside, they were stopped by security. She was led away. He was free to go.

Donald listened impassively to Mulder's confession of his adventure.

"You are a lost soul," he said. "Forever pretending to be bigger than you are. But oh so respectable nowadays."

"Indeed, respectability comes with age, thanks to hormonal decline."

The barman brought two more drinks. Several dollars per sip.

"Lost soul, lost soul," Mulder echoed. "Aren't we both lost souls? In Paris you didn't really belong with the comrades, and over on the coast you still don't belong, not with the whites and not with the coloureds. You live in the kind of country you don't want, and which doesn't really want you either."

Donald sighed. "If only I could be proud. Proud, like those black waiters over there, then I'd be able to throw myself into the celebrations of our new-fangled national holidays, I'd dance in the street, cheer for my president. I haven't had much opportunity to feel proud of my country. Yes, there was Mandela's release, the first general election, the reconciliation movement, but the hatchet has not been properly buried yet, revenge and retribution still hold sway. You can see it in the blacks with new money – now it's our turn! And in the whites retreating to their bunkers – unwillingly."

A cockroach scuttled along the plinth. Donald squashed it with the tip of his shoe. His expression was dour.

"Perhaps I'm too worried about the rise of a new kind of nationalism. My family venerated the wrong heroes when I was young: people like the Voortrekkers, who freed themselves by seizing other people's land, the Boer generals, the Paul Krugers, the Treghardts. And today? How can I be proud of corrupt leaders, of thousands of school children without textbooks, of insatiable greed and violence against immigrants?"

Mulder countered with a list of European evils. Were things so much better there?

"No," Donald said, "but at least in Europe you can live without guilt. Being white in South Africa means you're burdened with the past. You can deny it, but you'll be reminded of it anyway. In Europe you don't get beggars coming to your door. In Europe the third world is just another item on the news, and you don't have to empathise with illiterate black compatriots on a daily basis."

They wished each other a thicker skin, and conversed at length on the necessary freedom to make errors of judgement, however blatant. They spoke from experience.

Mulder escorted Donald to the exit. They strolled under the palm trees and, in parting, exchanged a left handshake – with the hand nearest to the heart, Boy Scout style.

The letter, the damn letter. He couldn't very well leave the country without having written to the pen-pal seeker. Why had he taken the card from the supermarket noticeboard in the first place? He had only robbed other people of the opportunity to show kindness to a man in prison – better people, people to whom charity was not a chore.

It would have to be a letter with some beauty to it, jail was ugly enough. The tone would be humane, but not sentimental, outspoken without being harsh, sincere but not condescending. Half-formed ideas floated around his head, pithy comments – his language was newly seasoned with Afrikaans, after all. No idea what sort of person would read his letter . . . a man whose interests were reading, writing and politics, according to the card, an educated man presumably, white or coloured. But it could just as well be some racist blabbermouth, some nasty little creep who raged against the world in general and despised a well-turned phrase. What was he getting himself into? Was this his guilty conscience playing up? Or a question of solidarity with the down-trodden? And wouldn't it be cruel to write just the one letter and leave it at that?

Mulder had no desire to put himself in anybody else's shoes. He wanted to write the kind of letter he himself would have wished to receive under the circumstances, which was like giving the kind of presents he wouldn't mind being given himself. He used to fanta-sise a lot about what it would be like to be arrested, interrogated, tortured, sent to prison. It could have happened, Marten could easily have found himself behind bars.

Mulder took a few sheets of hotel stationery from the leather folder on the writing table. Cream-coloured notepaper embossed with a small pink flag at the top. A guest staying at the country's most expensive hotel takes pity on a prisoner. How kind.

Dear friend, he wrote . . . Friend? Pen-pal? Or dumbo, blockhead, bloody fool?

> *How come you allowed yourself to get caught? How could you be so stupid as to end up spending part of your life between grey walls? My present view of walls – the walls of Table Mountain – is more atractive than yours. We have round-the-clock room*

service. I go to the courtyard to have lunch. You go to the court-
yard for fresh air. A twist of fate. When you're walking round
yours and looking up at your square of sky, tomorrow, say, shall
I come hovering overhead and throw you a rope ladder? Rescue
by Superman. I have always wanted to fly. Still dream of it every
night. But awake I find myself imprisoned in a leaden body. Yes,
even freedom is a prison.

Better scrap that last sentence. Bit too facetious.

Sometimes I feel myself a prisoner. An abstraction to me, reality
to you.

What was your crime? Some misdemeanor, I hope, some all
too human error. That would be easier for me to imagine. Money
that asked to be taken. A gun waiting to be used. Me, I have stolen.
And used a gun.

Self-indulgence. An intellectual with worldly pretensions. Used a
gun? Yes, for target practice. And too much of a wimp to slice the
head off a fish.

Fresh sheet. No more confessional stuff. Baring the soul wasn't
going to help the prisoner.

Dear Pen-Pal.
You are a prisoner in a country which I helped to liberate: as a
courier, cutting the last chains of slavery. How worthy that sounds.
I dreamed of being a hero, but it didn't work out that way. Too
scared. Too lazy, more like.

As a self-styled comrade I had high hopes of a free South Africa.
A country with civil rights for all, not an imitation of Europe, but
an African state that would make short shrift of all the existing
prejudices about the continent, with decent schools and enough

sense of national cohesion to grant a bunch of old whites some
space as well. No longer a passive victim, but a proactive nation
entitled to make its own mistakes, and to learn from them.

So many dreams, my friend . . . But freedom arrived. Only, free-
dom brought a lot of fear with it. The change came too quickly for
some, who suddenly had to share their space (and more) with
others, and who responded by erecting walls, higher than those
of your prison. Walls everywhere: around estates, around towns,
around private homes, around themselves. And no rope ladder of
escape. All they can see is their own shadow trembling on the
wall. At least the shadows are all the same colour.

Clichés. Into the bin. Third attempt.

Hi,

Ever since I took your card from that supermarket noticeboard I
have had you living in one of my brain cells. It took me a while to
realise why, but the fact is that your message triggered a long-
suppressed memory. Your incarceration reminded me of some-
body I had avoided thinking about for some years. Someone
with expert knowledge of captivity. His name was Duriez – a man
of many faces. In Paris he was known as the chief of Fraternité,
an organisation offering training to third-world exiles and
dissidents in anticipation of their return to their as yet unliber-
ated countries. Perfectly legal. He enjoyed the staunch support of
the Protestant church. But behind the scenes he trained a select
group of militants for active resistance. People with a mission,
and converts like me. South Africa, being the only country in the
world with racial segregation written into the constitution, had
top priority.

I did not much like Duriez, because he had too much in

common with my father (so I thought at the time). A short, cruel man, literally marked by the tribulations of his past. He could do no wrong in the eyes of my mentor in the resistance, a student a little bit older than me. He and I became friends only later.

Duriez had been held in five different prisons. He had a number tattooed on the inside of his arm: a souvenir of his "German adjournment", as he put it. The scars on both wrists stood for torture in Algiers, where he was involved in a communist resistance group. He was betrayed because he was a Jew, and as such too much of an outsider. After that he joined sides with the Palestinians. Another spell in prison: for showing more respect for Peking than for Mecca. The Mossad were after him. Russians ditto. Each country, each party, had carved a souvenir on his skin. He seized every opportunity of showing one or other of his scars, thereby transporting us to mould-infested cells in Algeria, the rat cages of Hebron, tiled cubicles without windows in Tel Aviv, or the airless fore-cabin of a Russian cargo ship off the coast of Cyprus. My father was also imprisoned in a fore-cabin (other ship, other ocean, other war), but he kept that to himself. Not so Duriez, he glorified imprisonment, and always came up with the same advice. You may find it interesting.

Prison is all in the mind. So is the crowbar. The problem is the other people. Prison director, guards, fellow inmates. The cellmate who rapes you. You are obliged to deal with people you hate, like in a bad marriage. They prey on you, try to cut you down. You suffer. You are in hell, but hell is other people, as the French philosopher Jean-Paul Sartre put it. (Duriez was always quoting him, especially the book entitled No Exit in English translation. You like reading, I gather from your card. You could apply for the book from the library.)

Books can set you free, and if you don't have a book, you can write one in your head. Imagine yourself free. Envisage a view on the other side of the wall. Stroke the rats, they are your pets. Your rapist is a one-night stand. The bunch of keys a carillon. The coarse fabric of your prison costume looks and feels like silk, the foul air coming from the dark corridors is the breeze billowing a ship's sail – take it as proof of wind, see it.

Tell lies you really believe in, forget the facts that don't suit you, just never recall them, or only for as long as absolutely necessary. Deny the existence of reality, while taking account of the reality of what you deny. It's the only way you'll survive (George Orwell, I believe, another of Duriez's heroes).

Self-deception, you will say. It takes neither effort nor practice, it is like eating and drinking. We deceive ourselves so that we may tolerate the other. We deceive one another to avoid the worst. Consciously or not. The lie is a product of our evolution. Placebo ergo sum.

I used to think him rather a twit, old Duriez, but now that I am writing all this down I think he may have had a point. Perhaps I was imprisoned between the walls of South Africa for too long.

P.S. Invent a future for yourself, and for your country. And don't complain about wasted time. Time cannot be wasted. Time just is.

That was over the top again, the calendar wisdom about time. But Mulder did not toss his letter into the wastepaper basket, he folded it and slipped it into a tissue-lined hotel envelope. He cut his tongue on the sharp edge of the flap as he licked the glued strip. "Doesn't hurt, doesn't hurt, it's just a kiss," he mumbled as he dropped the letter in the hotel mailbox.

Mulder lay back on the bed of his room, which had a view of Table Mountain through the open door to the balcony. He was glad to be alone. *Calme, luxe, volupté* . . . It was his last morning at the Cape. He turned the pages of the newspapers. Plenty of bloodshed and sport (good for sales), which he didn't dwell on. Behind all the gore glimmered a brighter future – the country cherished high hopes. Well, he was old enough to know that the higher you aim the deeper the disappointment. But a young country? Hope was all you had if you were poor. Cynicism was a luxury, just as his commitment – however sincere at times – had been in the past. He vowed to banish all feelings of moral outrage henceforward. You had to accept people as they were, strange as they might seem. Detachment, inspired by love, was what was needed. Imposing one's values on the rest of humanity was no good. Besides, if those first-world values really were that great then it was about time they were taken seriously at home.

He resolved to become even more of a people-watcher. Sit back and watch the bustle in the street. From sad to happy. Or vice versa. Oh, he couldn't wait for it to be winter, so he could take his morning stroll in the Luxembourg gardens and sit in the sun by the Orangerie during break time at the Lycée Montaigne, watch the girls, well-bred fillies every one, young Catherines, sharing park benches with unwashed tramps or black *nounous* in charge of white men's toddlers – the world at face value. Unjust. Beautiful, too, sometimes. That was what he would focus on, keep it in his sights as in the days of *la filature*. Being there by not being there. Yes, that was what it came down to, the outcome of his extended memory trip down old and distant lanes.

It was busy at the airport. Sunburnt faces and tattoos all around –
passengers waiting for the flight to Amsterdam. They had been
in Africa, and to show it they wore garish shirts and dreadlocks and
beads in their blonde hair. Mulder was glad he was flying to Paris.
But the French went on and on about game reserves.

He got himself an upgrade. Business class might well harbour
those worthy of several hundred years of penal servitude, but at
least he wouldn't have to rub elbows with the person sitting next to
him. Besides, you could get a glass of champagne in the first-class
lounge beforehand. He picked up a Dutch newspaper. Islam, lots of
Islam, and fear for the future.

The man beside him – Dutchman, good suit, loafers, signet ring,
respectable – leaned over. Mad about South Africa, he was, went
there every year: amazing country. "But," he said, putting his hand
on Mulder's arm, "I'm not too sure about the blacks getting to run
the place for real."

"That is the intention, yes," Mulder said.

"But it'll all go to pot."

Mulder said nothing. He was too old for this kind of conversation.

The man's flight was called. Mulder nodded goodbye. His hand
was a fist, ready to take up the cutter and hollow out a bible and
stuff the hole with a plastic bomb. Not as Marten, but as Mulder.

See? The desire to meddle was in his nature.

Cape Town, January 2009 – Paris, August 2010

ADRIAAN VAN DIS is a Dutch author with roots in what was the Dutch East Indies (now Indonesia). As a young man he studied Afrikaans at Amsterdam University. His novel *My Father's War*, translated into English by Ina Rilke in 2004, won a number of prizes in the Netherlands and was shortlisted for the IMPAC Award.

INA RILKE is the prize-winning translator of books by Cees Nooteboom, W. F. Hermans, Erwin Mortier, Louis Couperus, Hella Hasse and Otto de Kat.